THE APPRENTICE JOURNALS III: KIMIKIN

BY
J. MICHAEL SHELL

Published by
Dog Horn Publishing
45 Monk Ings, Birstall, Batley WF17 9HU
United Kingdom
doghornpublishing.com

ISBN 978-1-907133-93-0

Edited by
Steve Redwood

Cover by
Vincent Sammy

Typesetting by
Jonathan Penton

UK Distribution: NBN International
10 Thornbury Road
Plymouth
PL6 7PP
Telephone: 01752 202301
Email: cservs@nbninternational.com

Overseas Distribution: Printondemand-worldwide.com
9 Culley Court
Orton Southgate
Peterborough
PE2 6XD
Telephone: 01733 237867
Facsimile: 01733 234309
Email: info@printondemand-worldwide.com

THE
APPRENTICE
JOURNALS III:
KIMIKIN

TABLE OF CONTENTS

I
I am Kimikin

My father told me—many times—that Apprentices should keep up with their journals. He even bought me a book, which I'm sure was very expensive even though there were no words printed on its pages. "When you fill this one, I'll buy you another," he told me.

"Fill it?" I said. "There are hundreds of pages!"

"Then you'd better get started."

I was twelve when he gave me that book. Now I'm fifteen, and this is the first time I've written in it. Though he never said a word, or even asked if I'd started my journal, I always felt a little guilty that I hadn't. Now I feel *very* guilty, because I'm sure I've caused him much pain. And probably Mother, too, though I don't feel guilty at *all* about *her* pain.

My father is known by a number of names. To my mother he is Spearl—the name given him by *her* mother. A very few call him Thirest, but none of those are human. My grandmother on my mother's side—the Great Lady Pearl—named him Spearl when he wore another body, and was her son. Psychically, Pearl and Spaul (the Heroes of World) were *his* parents as well as *my* mother's. Physically, he is the Finished Apprentice Thirest, whose light now dwells with the Fierae.

If that all sounds confusing, imagine how it sounded to me growing up. Both my parents spoke of my grandparents—also wards of the Fierae, now—as *their* parents, which, of course, conjured images of incest (anathema to Apprentice rules). But things were explained, and I was assured that my genes were not compromised. As I say, it was confusing, but I always felt my parents' love, and that sufficed. As for my father's true name, it didn't matter to me. I've always called him Daddy.

The name they gave me is Kimikin. Daddy calls me Kimi. I was named for my other "grandmother" (maybe stepmother?), to whom I have no genetic link. But I know her well, and understand the perfect love she felt for my father when he wore his other skin. Daddy once told me that I *am* his Kimmy, returned so that he might know a different kind of love for her. I have always accepted that we return and live many lives. But I've seen Kimmy in Daddy's traces, and do not believe I am her. Perhaps I *was*, but not now. I am Kimikin, and though I allow my father (and *only* my father) to call me Kimi, I do not love him the way Kimmy did. The fact that I could *never* love a man the way Kimmy loved is the great bone that contends between Mother and me. She is very nearly desperate to see my "powers," as she says, passed on to a daughter— her granddaughter. But I am what I am and love who I love. If I am meant to have a child, one will spontaneously erupt from my body. Barring that, the aneke'lemental line ends with me.

I suppose I should, to begin this journal, say something about my childhood. Well, it was confusing in more ways than one. And since I haven't really figured it all out yet, I'll just leave it at that. Instead, I'll begin with the events that led me finally to start writing this—the events that caused me to run away from home...

Now that I think about it, that's pretty confusing, too. So let's just say Mother caught me in the barn with Lizabeth, who'd ridden on my back all the way from Smith's Crossing. I'd gone down there to get her in the morning, and would have had her back before dark if Mother hadn't come snooping. We were pretty much delectably flagrant when Mother walked in and yelled, "She's your gollam niece, Kimikin!"

"Watch your mouth, Mother!" I told her. "There's ladies present. And she's *not* my niece! I'd have to have been Spearl and Kimmy's daughter for her to be my niece!"

"Spearl was my *twin*!" she insisted.

"It's awful gollam flimsy, Mother," I insisted right back. "And anyway," I smiled, "we don't plan on having kids."

To make a long story short, I got locked in my room, and Mother flew Lizabeth back to the Crossing (once we were both dressed again, of course).

Even if my room had been made of pure glass, locking me in it was exercising futility. I'm gollam aneke'lemental, after all. So I filled up my pack with this and that (including this book), and hit the road (okay, the *lines*). I thought about heading south and liberating Lizabeth, but to tell the truth, I'd had enough of her, too. There's been a time or two lately when I'm sure I smelled boy on her.

Anyway, my so-called "niece" is way too old for me, being almost eighteen and all.

Trust me, "niece" had nothing to do with it, anyway. What Mother couldn't abide about Lizabeth was the fact that she's a *girl*. "It's one thing to *play*," she told me, "but you need to find a *mate*! Someone you can *mate with*! You have no idea the trouble the Fierae went through to plot this trace, to bring aneke'lementals into World."

"You can't plot traces, Mother! My namesake proved that!"

"What did I do to deserve such a willful brat!" she lamented.

"Well, let's see," I told her. "You had the hots for your twin brother, you built forbidden Ancient teck, and, oh yes, you set fire to a Finished Apprentice. I'd say I'm *well* deserved!"

Slam! Click! She locked me in and left to take Lizabeth home.

If Daddy hadn't been away, I might not have left. He always manages to cool me down, and Mother as well. But he was off on some Apprentice errand, and I was madder than a muley with bees in his hay.

I'd always wanted to go to Ginny, but had never been. Mother promised to take me there shopping once I'd "settled down a bit" (whatever that means). But until then, I was forbidden to travel north. Fug it! I strapped on my pack, stopped by the barn to grab a little jug of Daddy's Corn (*that* would settle me down a bit), and left. Heading *north*! Ginny, here I come!

II
Thirest's Journal
(continues)

Before Star and I left Thirest's bunker, I found his journal. Most of it was in loose pages, neatly gathered and sandwiched into a stiff, folded sheet of leather. But there was also a bound book full of mostly empty pages. Immediately, I perceived that it was sealed with elemental majick, and the only hands capable of opening it were the ones I now wore—Thirest's. Only the first quarter of it had been filled. These were the last of Thirest's musings. Considering the many blank pages, I believed his end came upon him unexpectedly, and I was anxious to read those last entries. Though all of what I read was interesting and insightful, it was the last page that fixed my attention:

"The Fierae are calling me. It is far too soon for me to join, or even converse, with them again, but I know I have no choice. The ground charge is waiting, and a storm will come soon. I have spoken with her through my calmed sea while still in my body. She is hard to understand, though not as sleepy as she should be. Sometimes I think it isn't so much that *I* don't understand, as that the Fierae themselves are in some way unsure of what they tell me.

"As best I can comprehend, there will come a time when I will leave my body here, preserved by my beloved Spaul, to be filled at some future date by the light of another Apprentice. This may occur sooner rather than later, as I cannot imagine surviving this next joining.

"I hope it is Spaul who will inhabit my body. Wouldn't that be an irony!"

After this sentence, Thirest drew a simple little face wearing a smile. I found it curious.

"If it is you, Spaul, reading this, I hope you find love. I hope I didn't frighten you away from it. I've always known it would be a girl you will seek. I hope you find her, and that she loves you as much as I do."

I wondered if I would tell my father about these lines in Thirest's journal if I ever saw him again in his light-body. But, no, I wouldn't. If Thirest wanted him to know, he could tell him himself.

For all these years, I have kept no journal. I saw no point, as the New Apprentices need no finding or training. Also, and this may sound strange, every time I picked up a pen and saw it in someone else's hand, I simply could not write. I even discovered that my handwriting was different. But when I found that it matched, exactly, the handwriting in Thirest's journal, I made a decision. I decided to continue Thirest's journal, and write it in his name. Call it payment for the body I've used these past dozen years. As Spearl I had written *so much*! I would let the writings of Spearl the Historian end, and the Journal of Thirest the Apprentice continue.

III
Thirest's Journal
(per Spearl)

How do I describe the love I have for Star—even to myself? As her brother, I loved her more dearly than I am able to say. While she was gone all those years, I missed her terribly. Though I look down and see these hands that are not my own, I am still Spearl. Sometimes, when I love Star, I am very much aware of that fact. It is strange, but to be perfectly honest, it has often added a touch of the erotic. I actually asked Star once if it affected her the same way. "When I love you, I am whole," she said. "It feels more natural to me than breathing."

Star and I have made our home at Grandfather Tool's farm. For a long time we were there exclusively. Kimikin was conceived at Thirest's bunker, and very soon we were a family of three. Kimi was not a fully aware and talking baby the way Star and I were, but in a year, she spoke fluently, and at two, she could call and ride the lines.

Shortly after that, we began taking her to Smith's Crossing to play with her "cousins" (who were actually, technically, nieces and nephews on Star's genetic side), and to interact with the great variety of people who come through and stay at the now bustling inn. By the time she was five, Kimi had found her way into traces of knowledge (and, I think, mine) and could carry on a conversation that even the most educated might struggle to follow. Kimikin was a New Apprentice, but she was also aneke'lemental, which caused as many problems as it did delights.

Blitz once told me that my life-mate Kimmy would return in my daughter, but I never saw it. Kimikin is something of a wild-child, which is a problem for her mother, but to me, secretly, always a delight. What also became apparent was that she, like many Apprentices, is drawn to her own gender. I had no problem with this, as I had known it to be natural and common among Apprentices all my life (*lives*). Star, on the other hand, cannot abide this fact of our daughter's nature. Her greatest fear is that the aneke'lemental line will end.

Though I've said I never really saw Kimmy in Kimikin, their sexual appetites do bear a similar ring. Of course, a lot of that has to do with the very nature of the New Apprentices. As the male Apprentices used to seek out and engage in Fierae love, the elementals now seek and enjoy female Apprentice encounters. Apparently, they encourage such engagements. Vigorously.

Though I always knew the *words* of The One Certainty— "Love is Above the Rules"—my involvement with the Fierae has shown me that there are *many* rules that love is above. Although I am Kimikin's father, and would keep her from harm, I can't see her loving as harmful—except, perhaps, to her mother's frame of mind.

IV
Not Lonely Alone

While Mother demanded, commanded, insisted and forbade, Daddy asked (he's so *smart!*). Spearl, in both incarnations, had been saddled with some very strong women. He'd learned from his mistakes, and theirs. Mother had forbidden me to travel north. She'd take me to see Ginny and the Village of Ilsa (once her own Star City) when I'd "earned her trust," whatever that meant.

But I think she knew the only reason I acceded to these demands (until recently, of course) is because Daddy had *asked* me to. Mother either knew better than to forbid me riding the lines altogether, or Daddy had asked her not to. More than likely it was the latter. For the most part, Mother does what he asks.

But all bets were off as I took a pull of what Daddy calls, "Tool's Recipe," caught my breath (it's *strong* Corn), and called up lines...heading *north*. I thought about hitting the beach first, but I'd been many times and was hot for something *new*. At first I had the Zephs blowing me pretty quickly—I wanted to get to Ginny and see some *people*. See some *girls*. But before long I slowed my pace. "Take a look around," I told myself. "This is all *new!*"

At some point I stopped altogether. A gentle breeze was blowing through the trees to the west. I'd been riding over the old Ninety-five, but those trees seemed to be calling. Suddenly, it dawned on me that I was truly *alone* for the first time in my life. It also occurred to me that I should probably be lonely, but I wasn't. I *liked* this being alone. Then I realized that the calls (insistences?) of my body weren't bothering me. As a rule, I'm a creature with pretty big horns. But I found myself glad to be done with Lizabeth. My passions were calm (and if they *hadn't* been, I wasn't above doing something about it all by myself right there in the grass on the Ninety-five). It was a relief. It was a *wonderment!* Slowly, arms spread and twirling with my newfound freedom, I made my way into the lush woods, listening to the gentle song the breeze was singing in there.

Sitting with my back to a fine old sycamore, I took another pull of my grandfather's "recipe." I knew to be careful with it. I'm not saying I've never been drunk, but when you're aneke'lemental all sorts of things (usually *embarrassing* things) can happen if you get beyond the point of being able to neutralize it. Trust me, I know.

One of the cuter examples of this (and one of the few I'll relate) was the time when I was eleven and discovered Corn for the first time. Daddy chuckled, but Mother was not amused when they caught me, naked, riding our big, fuzzy sheep around the yard. It's a vague memory, but a fond one. It felt good.

Daddy only had the one sheep—somebody had given it to him after he'd healed their daughter's two broken legs. The sheep disappeared shortly thereafter, and Mother claimed it ran away. But I also remember eating meat I'd never tasted before right after Snowy "ran away." Sometimes that family came to visit us, and their daughter and I became friends. Her name was Olli. But that's another story (that also involved Corn and didn't end well).

Corking the jug, I reached into my pack and found my little pipe and pouch of ganja. I grew that Maria myself, and trust me, being aneke'lemental I can grow some serious bud. I don't know if Lizabeth will miss me much, but she'll sure as helluva miss my weed.

Corn and Maria made love in my brain, and I dozed off (I think) sitting against that tree. I'm not a shykik the way Mother is (thank Jess), but I do occasionally have shykik dreams, and the dream I had amongst those trees sure felt like one.

Shykik dreams are *very* real, *very* bright and colorful. If you pay attention and can figure them out, they'll tell you something important—something that might happen, or maybe show you someone you're going to meet and tangle up with.

If it *was* a shykik dream, I didn't think I'd be meeting up with any of the characters that inhabited it, as they were some kind of Fairae, straight out of myth.

In the dream, I was sitting in the dark right there against that tree, still all nice and buzzed up from my ganja. I saw tiny lights darting around in the night, and immediately thought of the tales Mother used to tell me when I was little. Tales she embellished with elemental majick, which rapt my attention. It looked so much like one of Mother's trick-laden stories that I actually thought she'd caught me and was somewhere nearby. "Mother?" I said tentatively. Then I heard giggling. *"Who's there?"*

When I called out, those tiny, flickering lights began to gather around me, and I could see that they were winged creatures about the size of big dragonflies. When they drew close, I realized they were tiny girls. "Gollam!" I said.

"Gollam!" they all repeated in squeaky little voices. Then they giggled again.

"What *are* you?" I asked.

One of the—I don't know—*Fairaes*, I guess, flew up to me quicker than a tendril of lectric, swatted my nose, and said, "What are *you*? And how did you get to this side?"

Her voice was so tiny and high, like a tinkling sound, that I said, "Speak up. I can barely hear you."

As soon as I said that she began spinning furiously...and *growing*! With her arms out, as if to keep her balance, she stopped her spinning and landed on her feet. Now she was all of three feet tall, nude (delightfully so), and still vaguely glowing. "Can you hear me now?" she asked.

"Gollam, you're cute," I told her.

The other, still tiny girls all giggled again, but the grown one said, "Forget it. You're human and you stink!" Again, the others laughed. "Now tell how you come to be here. Humans can't cross, it's not possible. Even *we* don't go back and forth anymore."

"I'm afraid I don't know what you're talking about," I told her. "And I *don't stink*!"

"Oh," she said, tossing her head back and rolling her eyes, "but you *do*! Human is an *awful* smell!"

"I'm not exactly human," I told her. "I'm aneke'lemental."

"Really?" she asked, seeming suddenly impressed. "I guess you don't stink *too* bad. But you still haven't told us how you got here."

I shrugged my shoulders and said, "Rode the lines? Walked?"

"But how did you *cross*?" she insisted.

This girl with the dragonfly wings wasn't making any sense, and I was suddenly feeling quite dizzy. "Are you a Fairae?" I managed to ask.

"How insulting!" the girl huffed. "We're FireSprites! Fairae are nowhere near as bright...*or pretty*!"

In an indignant instant, she spun herself tiny, swatted my nose again, then the whole gaggle of them darted away and were gone. I woke up rubbing my nose, which made me laugh and say out loud, "No, Kimikin, a Fairae did *not* slap your nose!" Then I could have sworn I heard a tiny voice say, "FireSprite!"

V
Returning to Trouble

In Thirest's body, I am the Apprentice I always wanted to be, and more. The "more" part is the Fierae enhancement Blitz gave me when he died at Thirest's bunker. Star believes I may even be eneke'lemental, but how does one tell? I certainly don't have the abilities she has, and I've a feeling Kimikin may be potentially stronger than either of us...maybe than *both* of us. I've seen signs.

Now I've come home to find Kimikin missing. Star is frantic and angry at once—conditions she does not handle well. When she came back from the Fierae, Star was certainly different in many respects. Calmer, to say the least, and being with me, now—being "whole," as she puts it—usually keeps her that way. But just as she used to incite our mother to bouts of what I will generously call aggravated passion, Kimikin similarly ignites (poor choice of words?) Star's.

"I caught her with Lizabeth!" Star told me angrily.

"They're friends," I said in the calmest voice I could muster.

Star's eyes sparked into lavender flames, and I knew what was coming. "I *caught them...*" she began furiously, but I stopped her.

"Please don't put that picture in my head," I said softly. "She's my daughter."

"And Lizabeth?" Star shouted at me. "How about *her* picture in your head?"

"Jealousy?" I asked, forcing a frown that may have betrayed me and turned to a grin-of-sorts.

"Yes!" she screamed. "I'm a jealous, angry, horrible woman! And I've driven my daughter away! I can't feel her, or hear her! It's as if she's left World!"

Seeing the tears in Stars eyes, I said, "She's strong."

Then Star really scared me. The flames left her eyes and she dropped to her knees sobbing. "I've lost her," she wept, "and World will lose aneke'lementals."

Taking her by the shoulders, I stood her. She still looked so very young to be talking about such things. Gently I kissed her and said, "Neither of those things has happened. In the morning, we'll go find Kimikin."

"How?" she asked in a pleading voice. "I can't *feel* her. I don't know where she's gone."

"Of course you do," I told her. "She's gone north."

"I forbade..." she began.

"Exactly!" I interrupted.

"She's willful," Star pouted.

"Ha!" I exclaimed. "The pot casting aspersions on the kettle!"

"Calling the kettle black," she corrected.

"Seems to me, Father and Mother had a daughter so willful she built a lectric farm."

"Which wasn't such a bad thing, other than the coal," she smiled, calming considerably. "I hear they're farming small amounts of lectric in Ilsa now with waterwheels and windmills."

"What *is* it about that place?" I asked her. "Always *something* going on there."

"Even when it was Tara," she said, her eyes gone distant, "good dwelled with the evil."

"Tomorrow we'll find Kimikin," I said, bringing her out of her reverie. "Maybe she went to the beach."

"It worries me so that I can't feel her."

"Maybe Lizabeth knows where she is."

"I took Lizabeth back to the Crossing myself. She wasn't even embarrassed or contrite!"

"It was *play*, Star. You're becoming awfully gollam parochial."

"I am *not* parochial. I simply want a granddaughter. And I prefer not to have to see my daughter in such a flushed tangle with another girl!"

"You did that to yourself."

"Did *what* to myself?" she asked, trying to hide a mischievous grin.

"You knew what they were doing out there. You should have left them alone."

"I know," she said, contritely. "When we find her, I'll apologize. Then I'll take her to Ginny and surround her with boys!"

"You're bad," I told her.

"And you've known that for a very long time," she smiled.

I didn't expect Star to sleep much that night, but she surprised me. She looked so peaceful (finally) and pretty that I lay there, propped on an elbow, watching her. I was about to give that up (as I found myself suddenly *wanting* her) when she...*changed*. Right before my eyes, she became *opaque*, and I noticed the cover over her starting to settle into the bed. Then she was *gone*! Just for an instant, she disappeared as the blanket settled onto the bed. I was about to shout when that blanket inflated again with Star, whole and solid, under it. In a moment, her eyes blinked open, she yawned once, and, looking up at my startled face, said, "What a dream I've just had!"

"Shite!" was all I could think to say.

"What's wrong?" she asked.

"I'm not sure," I told her. "Tell me about your dream."

"I saw Kimikin and another girl, you know, the way I found her with Lizabeth. And one of them had *wings*, or maybe both, I'm unsure. The wings must represent her flying the coop, so to speak. The other, well, it's been on my mind. Strange how such things assault us in our sleep."

"You disappeared," I said.

"No," she told me, "I was standing in a woods, watching."

"I *mean*, you disappeared out of this bed! I was looking at you, and you just vanished."

"Seems *you* had a dream as well."

"I wasn't dreaming." I said. "For a second or two, you were *gone*."

Star sat up and her eyes grew wide. "I'm hungry!" she said with a surprised look, as if that were somehow unusual.

"So?" I asked.

"I need liver, Spearl! I'm *that* kind of hungry! And I'm hungry for *you*! I need liver and applesauce and a serious bedding!"

"In that order?" I asked with a smile.

With*out* a smile, Star said, "No!" and jumped me like an animal—a predator—in heat. Without fanfare (or foreplay) she devoured her prey.

VI
Blue Lips and Breakfast

I slept against the sycamore the rest of that night. Though my dreams weren't shykik, they did involve that cute little creature, and were quite...well...you know. I awoke to dawn's light, and noticed for the first time that I was facing a tiny clearing, almost perfectly round. There were mushrooms growing in it, and some of them were the *right kind* of mushrooms (which usually grow in cow patties). You can always be sure by snapping the stems. If they bleed blue, they're the right kind.

Having experienced those mushrooms, I can tell you that they're another thing an aneke'lemental should be careful with (actually, *nobody* should take them lightly). There are several small, very scorched cedar trees down by the ridge pond that I once thought were Masons in pointy hats coming to take me across the sea (from another of Mother's enhanced tales). Lizabeth and I were "camping out" when that happened—a couple of years ago, before the petting got so heavy. It was lucky she didn't get hurt. She'd eaten those 'shrooms, too (the whole thing was her idea), and had wandered off by the time I started burning up those "Masons."

Still, I picked a few before I left the clearing and put them in my pack (waste not, as they say). I was about to head back out to the Ninety-five when I noticed a big mushroom, torn to pieces, by the tree where I'd slept. It seemed strange to me, and it was then that I noticed the bitter taste in my mouth.

I have a tiny little mirror, a treasure that used to belong to the Great Lady Pearl. Daddy gave it to me when he gave me the blank journal. I fished it out of my pack, and, sure enough, could see a pale blue stain about my lips. But I *hadn't* eaten any... hadn't even *found* them yet. I don't scare easily, but this, not to mention the "FireSprites," had me concerned. Was I losing my mind, doing things and not remembering? For just a moment (and it passed quickly), I thought about running home to Daddy. Then I remembered Mother would be there, too.

As soon as I cleared the trees, I called to the Zephs and had them cocoon me up about a hundred meters. I don't know why, but it makes me feel safe, and anyway I wanted to look around. Off to the northwest, I could see the foothills of the First Mountains. What a magnificent sight! "That's where I'm going!" I said aloud. I'd hunt girls in Ginny *after* I visited those hills.

Unfortunately, I'd have to do some hiking. There's a trick to riding lines over a forest, and if you aren't good at it, you can fall. Mother can do it, and taught me to sort-of do it, but I really should have paid better attention to her lessons. It's tricky. I looked out over the forest and found a route that would take me through some lightly wooded areas—very nearly clearings. I could ride over those safely enough, and hike through the more heavily wooded areas. Yes! I was stoked!

Though I can go a long time without eating (especially if I don't majick too much), I do get hungry. Daddy and I—and Mother, too, sometimes—did a lot of camping, and I know how to clean and cook a hen or a rabbit, or even a mush rat (though they're definitely not my favorite thing to eat). I searched through Zeph eyes and saw a peahen thrashing around in some bramble. I dropped down on it and said, "Would you mind being breakfast?"

Her light was strained, and I knew before I heard her that she wasn't enamoured of the idea. "I've a clutch of eggs, four on the nest! Who will care for my chicks?"

"I'll tell you what," I told her. "Give me two of your eggs for breakfast, and I'll leave you in your body. Two chicks will be easier to look after, anyway."

"Yes, m'lady," she said. "That's fair. If it weren't for the chicks, I'd gladly give you my flesh. Maybe I'd come back a fox!"

"There are things that kill foxes as well, you know," I told her.

"Yes, m'lady. It's a dog-eat-dog world."

I swapped the peahen two eggs for her life, and built a fire. I keep a tiny pot in my pack, in which I boiled them. "Thank you for your flesh, little chicks-that-never-were," I said before I ate them. I also hoped, for the mother hen's sake, that the other two hatched.

With my belly full, I dipped a cloth in the hot water from the eggs, and wiped my mouth. When I saw that blue come off on the cloth, I felt another little shiver of fear. But I shook it off. "You're gollam aneke'lemental, Kimikin!" I said. "Something should be afraid of *you*!"

The map I'd made in my head had me hiking northwest for about twenty klicks, then I could ride for almost thirty. I shouldered my pack and headed into the dimmer light of the forest. I was fed, happy, and my horns were still sheathed! All I had to do was keep walking (and *not* start missing Daddy).

VII
Fish, a Fox,
and a Change of Heart

The second half of my twenty-klick hike had all been uphill. By the time I made it to the lightly wooded area, it was late afternoon. I'd been taking my time and enjoying the beauty, especially after little puffs from my pipe. I could have risen high in a Zeph cocoon, and fallen down lines across those next thirty klicks of light forest in a flash. But I decided to spend the night where I was, and ride through glorious dawn.

A narrow, though relatively deep, stream was running close by, so I called out some brimlets and a fat perch. Once cleaned, I skewered them onto green hickory twigs. They were roasting over my little fire when I heard a small fox peering out through a bush. "Might I have the heads when you're finished, little lady?"

"You're *awfully* bold," I told him (and he *was*), "letting me hear you like this. What if I decide to eat *you*?"

"Surely you wouldn't want a stringy thing like me when you have such a fine catch of fishes."

Though I've conversed with the light of many animals—mostly, of course, before I *ate* them—I'd never had one initiate a conversation. They just don't *do* that! And this fox had called me "little lady." From his perspective, I should have been *very big* lady. Also, he had to be able to tell I'm aneke'lemental (animals always know). Usually when they realize that they call me "m'lady," in deference to my Fierae heritage.

There was something not right about this fox, something not natural. Intrigued, I decided to investigate. "Come sit by my fire," I told him. "Keep me company and I'll let you have the heads."

Without hesitation, the fox crept out of his bush and plopped down next to my fire. "You're brave," I told him. "Most foxes are afraid of fire."

"Oh, I'm petrified," his light said. "But I really want those fish heads."

"Are you afraid of *me*?" I asked. "Afraid of humans?"

"Are you human?" his light said with a smile.

"Are you a fox?" I asked.

When I said that, the fox—not his light, mind you, but the *fox himself—smiled*! It frightened me so much that I woke with a start, and found myself sitting against a tree watching my fish burn. I dug out the little jug of Corn and took a good pull. "Shite!" I said, catching my breath. "I've got to quit dozing off like that!" I also needed to quit having mushroomy, shykik dreams!

I'm not dumb. I saw the connection between my fox dream and the conversation I'd had with the peahen. But what really disturbed me as I sat picking at what was left of my fish, was the fact that *everything* in that dream, except the fox, was right there in front of me. The bush he'd come skulking out of was exactly as it had been in the dream. The light of day, my fire, the position of my fish on their sticks! I even started looking around for footprints, but the ground was leaf-strewn and mulchy. I checked the bush, but found no fur. It was all very curious. In the end, I had to shrug it off as nothing more than a dream.

Even so, it freaked me out some, and I decided not to spend the night at that particular location. I had a bit of daylight left, and would walk a little farther into the lightly wooded area. In the morning, I'd call lines and make some time.

After walking no more than a klick, I found a sandy little clearing that would be soft under my blanket, and give me a lovely view of the stars. I was still a little spooked, and decided to start another fire. But in the middle of gathering wood, I changed my mind. I was not going to be a scaredy cat. What would Daddy say?

Then it hit me, full-on and unrelenting. *I missed Daddy!* He'd been gone for three days before I left, and a great big knot of hurt suddenly formed in my belly. Then I realized he probably had that same pain, and I couldn't bear the thought that I was the cause. "You're a stupid, stupid girl, Kimikin!" I said.

If only I could speak in his thoughts and tell him I was safe. But I'm no good at that from farther than a klick or so. I'd been blocking Mother from finding me since I left. I *could have* let her in for a sec, just to see I was safe, but I was afraid she'd catch my thought to turn tail for home. I didn't want to give her the satisfaction.

But that's exactly what I planned to do in the morning. I'd hike back the way I came. At least it would be downhill. Then unrelenting got the best of me and I allowed Mother in for a single nannysecond. "Safe," was all I let her hear.

VIII
Our Search Begins

Star ate liver again early that morning. I was still concerned about her disappearing act in bed that night, not to mention the nearly vicious love that ensued. "What could have drained you so?" I asked as she spooned applesauce.

"Some kind of very strong majick," she said with her mouth full. She was eating fast, wanting to be off to find Kimikin. I smiled when applesauce ran down her chin—she was so cute. She caught me smiling and wiped her face. "There's no time for that," she insisted.

"Time for what? Can't I just smile at you?"

"I know that smile," she scowled.

"You didn't mind that smile last night."

"That wasn't...*right*, last night, Spearl. It wasn't *me*. Maybe once, a long time ago..." For a moment I thought I saw tears, then she bucked up and said, "Let's go! I want my daughter. Something's terribly wrong, and I want her home. I want her safe! I want to spank her with a hickory switch!"

"There'll be none of that," I said sternly.

"I know," she said, and now there *were* tears. "I don't even know why I said it. I want to hold her in my arms and tell her I'm sorry. Dear Jess, let me find her today and I'll fetch Lizabeth for her myself."

I took Star in my arms. She stopped herself crying and said, "Let's go. I'm a stupid, stupid woman, Spearl."

"You're a *lovely* woman, and a good mother," I told her. "You just make mistakes now and then, like everybody else—including Kimikin. There'll be no spankings, but she's going to get a talking to once we get her home. Apparently, she took a little jug of the recipe with her when she left."

"I wish you'd stop making that and just make wine," Star said.

"Grandfather would come back and haunt us!" I smiled.

"I miss him," Star sighed.

"I miss Kimikin," I told her. "Let's go!"

27

We headed for the most logical place to start—the Ninety-five. Though Star could ride lines over wooded areas—an impressive trick—Kimi never really got the hang of it. Knowing she'd seek excitement, we decided to head toward Ginny.

Star agreed, and wanted to make a mad dash for that now burgeoning village, but I slowed her and said, "We need to take our time. We should look for signs of her along the way. She's smart, and may expect us to hunt for her in Ginny."

"Maybe she *wants* us to find her," Star said, and I couldn't tell if those were wind-tears or sad-tears in her eyes.

"At *some* point," I told her. "But she has a jug of courage and obstinacy with her, so I wouldn't expect that right away."

"She'll miss *you*," Star said, as those tears began streaming from her eyes.

"She'll miss us both," I told her. At some point, I added in my thoughts.

Star slowed us enough that we could be very aware of our surroundings. If Kimi stopped anywhere and put her feet on the ground, Star would see it. Or *would* she, as distraught and upset as she was?

With that in mind, I started keeping all my attention focused on the ground that passed beneath us, and to the sides as far as my peripheral vision would allow. Our passage was becoming a map in my head, but we were still going pretty fast. Some time after noon, I said, "Stop!"

"What is it?" Star asked. "What did you see?"

"Something," I told her. "I need to go over it, slow it down in my mind so I can see. And I'm hungry. What did you bring to eat?"

"I brought water," Star answered.

"Not even a biscuit?" I asked.

"We'll take Kimikin to eat in Ginny," she told me. "Now what did you see?"

As I sat reviewing my map of our passage, Star dug a wineskin out of her pack, chilled, and handed it to me. I took a few gulps of the cold water. "You could have at least brought wine," I told her.

"Find my daughter and I'll buy you a gallon in Ginny. Then I'll take you to a room and do wonderful things to your drunken body."

"*Hey!* Wait!" I said, finally seeing what must have caught my attention. "Several klicks back—I'm really focused on it—can you see?"

I could feel Star enter my thoughts, and a second later she said, "That's her! She stopped and walked west into the woods. How did I miss that?"

"You're a worried mama," I told her. "Not to mention probably still anemic."

"I'm fine," she insisted, grabbing the wineskin and tossing it into her pack. "Let's go!"

Very quickly, we made our way back to the disturbed place in the grass. "In there," Star pointed, and before long we came to a little round clearing. "She sat against that sycamore," Star told me. Then she teared up and said, in a pitiful voice, "She slept there."

"It's alright," I said, putting an arm around her, and wishing we'd brought more liver with us. Star was *not* fine.

It was then that I noticed the broken mushroom near where Kimi had slept. Unfortunately, Star saw it, too. "Oh, no!" she cried out, bending to pick up a piece of the mushroom. "She can't handle this, Spearl! *What have I driven my baby to do?*"

Star lost it completely, dropping to her knees and crying hysterically into her hands. I was sure now she needed to eat. Casting around through Zephrae eyes, I located a peahen sitting on a nest nearby. "I'm afraid I'm going to have to ask you for your body," I told her light.

"But I have two eggs on the nest," she answered. "Who'll look after my chicks?"

"I'll need your eggs as well. My life-mate needs food badly."

"I guess I just wasn't meant to live," she told me. "Maybe I'll come back as a fox."

I scooted the hen out of her body. As her light left, it said, "Two Fierae-humans in one day! Where are they all coming from?"

I seriously wanted to know what she meant by that, but it was too late. Her light was gone, and there was no bringing it back. I summoned Gryn from my pack and made short work of cleaning the bird. As it cooked, I made Star eat the liver and the two eggs raw.

It was obvious that Kimikin had hiked northwest from there. Where was she going? By the time we'd eaten, it was late afternoon. Star was sitting against the tree where Kimi had slept. I'd never seen her so sad and distraught. "We'll camp here and then find her in the morning," I said.

Star wanted to argue, but the insistent look on my face, and probably her own obvious weakness, kept her silent. Or perhaps it was something else—the something that suddenly made her go transparent. Then her eyes closed and she disappeared for several seconds. When she reappeared, she was obviously asleep, but her eyes blinked open and she said, "A fox!"

"That's what the peahen said," I told her. "Tell me, Star."

"First tell me what the peahen said," she insisted.

"It said it might come back as a fox, and that there seemed to be an awful lot of Fierae-humans coming through here."

"Kimikin?"

"Tell me what you saw."

Star's face instantly filled with fear, which was something I'd never seen. Not like this. "A fox is stalking our daughter," she said, her chin quivering.

I sat down and hugged her to me. "Then the fox is in danger," I told her.

"It isn't a fox," she said softly. "Its paws became hands."

"It was a dream, Star. How do you feel? Maybe in the morning you should fly home and let me find Kimikin."

"No, Spearl!" she said adamantly. "You may need me." Then she started crying again and said, "Please don't make me go!"

"I'd never *make* you," I told her.

"But you *could*," she wept.

"Well, I won't. Did this dream make you hungry?"

"Let's just say I'm glad you fed me so well."

"And the *other* kind of hungry?"

"I'm fighting it for all I'm worth right now, Spearl. I will *not* let it have its way with me again."

"What if *I* have my way with you?" I whispered.

"*Please* don't, Spearl. If you start I'll beg you to...to *hurt* me."

When she said that a terrible fear ran through me. Not knowing what else to do, I rocked her in my arms, and sang her one of Kimmy's old lullabies. She was tense and shaking for a good while. Then suddenly she relaxed, held me away by the shoulders, and said, with her eyes wide and smiling, "She's *safe!*"

IX
Fear and Ecstasy
(not in that order)

I was dreaming that Mother was forcing me to eat beets (which I *hate*), stuffing them into my mouth. Then I opened my eyes and saw my clearing bathed in what must have been the light of a full moon. But when I looked up, the starry night was moonless. "Back *again?*" I heard a tiny voice say.

I saw a light spinning out in the trees, then the little winged girl stepped into my clearing. *"How?"* she insisted, stomping her pretty, bare foot.

"How what?" I asked her.

"Are you *crossing*? Are there more of you coming? We really don't want you here, you know. You're going to make me have to report!" she said, placing her hands on her hips for emphasis.

"Well," I said, standing up. "You're just so pretty, I couldn't stay away."

When I said that, she blushed a blush that actually *glowed*. Then she said, shyly, "You'd probably be pretty, too, if you weren't wearing those obscene clothes. Doesn't it embarrass you?"

"No," I told her. "But I wouldn't be embarrassed to take them off, either."

"Well!" she said, her hands back on her hips.

Without thinking twice I shucked myself bare, then knelt close to my new, winged friend. "What's your name?" I asked.

"I am Claireth," she told me, "of the Clan Fiereste."

"*What* are you?" I persisted.

"A FireSprite! How many times must I tell you?" she harrumphed.

"But what *is* a FireSprite?" I pressed.

"We are HalfFire. Half luminous beings, half creature. You've a bit of Fire in *you*, don't you?" she asked.

"I have Fierae in me," I told her.

"Yes," she said, looking at me intently. "I see that now. But you've a lot of human in you as well, and all humans have a touch of the luminous. They just can't seem to realize it. Now, what is *your* name?"

"I'm Kimikin," I told her.

When I said that, Claireth's face went very dreamy. Then she smiled suggestively and said, "That's a cutie pie name. I'd just love to play with a HalfFierae girl called Kimikin. Now that I know it, your name spreads over you like honey! It almost makes up for having no wings." When she said that she blushed again, as if pointing it out embarrassed her. With a smile of my own, I leaned in and kissed her. "You've a little bitter on your tongue," she whispered. "Let me lick it off for you."

If *that* was a dream, it left me naked and sweating on my blanket. No! I'd been seriously played with—I could still feel it like an afterglow threatening to orgasm again. "What the *helluva*?" I said, sitting up in that lit-moon light. Then I noticed my pack. Someone had rummaged through it. There was also a bitter taste in my mouth, and I noticed pieces of mushroom beside me. I whispered, "Please, Jess, take away my fear."

When the 'fraidy cat subsided, I looked around and saw little paw prints in the sand. They came right up to my blanket, then— and believe me, fear came back with a vengeance—I saw a human hand print that was not my own!

Fear had the better of me now. I threw on my clothes, stuffed everything back in my pack, and summoned a Zeph cocoon. Up a hundred meters or so, I called lines heading southeast over the heavy forest. I was *not* hiking back through there. I wanted to go home, *now*! I tried to remember everything Mother had told me about riding lines over trees, then dropped down onto them. For at least a few klicks all was well. But sure enough the lines flickered, and down I went without any wings!

X
Dangerous Situation

I stayed awake watching Star sleep for quite a while. I didn't want her disappearing again, though, of course, I hadn't a clue how to stop it if she did. I must have dozed off for a bit, but I woke with a start and saw that Star was no longer beside me. "Star?" I called. She didn't answer.

I got up and had Terrae and Naiadae cooperate to light the clearing. That kind of majick is more phosphorescent glow than serious lighting, but at least I could see a bit. "Star!" I called, looking through the trees around the clearing. Eventually I looked back to our blankets and saw her lying there, just beginning to wake.

As soon as she opened her eyes, Star moaned and cried out in anguish. "He's stalking her! He'll steal my baby!"

I grabbed her into a hug, as she was shaking terribly. "The small girl, again!" she said, her voice on the verge of hysteria. Then her eyes grew wide and she said, "They both have wings and are flying and playing at love! Kimikin's wings disappeared! She's falling! My baby is falling!"

This was dangerous! Star was majick-starved, and in a state of shock. I needed to be stuffing her with raw liver, but I couldn't have gathered what she needed from dozens of peahens. I knew what I needed to do, and hoped I could manage it.

Star's eyes were losing awareness. I was afraid consciousness would go next. "Star!" I shouted, trying to keep her with me. "Climb up on my back! Now!"

Somehow, I got her piggy-backed. Then I cocooned us and rose up into the still dark morning. I called lines heading due east and shouted, "Star! Can you charge my hands? Concentrate! Spearl wants you to charge his hands!"

I dropped us onto the lines, unable to tell if she'd protected my hands. If not, I'd find out the hard way at the end of our ride.

When I took over Thirest's body, I also inherited his Finished Apprentice talent. Then Blitz died, and bequeathed me his "blood," which enhanced those already impressive skills.

34

I had a windscreen in front of us, a howl of Zephres behind, and we were traveling toward the sea at an incredible speed. It was still dark, and I was very lucky the surf contained a good bit of phosphorescence or I'd have never seen it and stopped us in time.

I left Star sitting in the sand staring into nothingness. In a minute, I had two markaral flouncing on the shingle. I willed Gryn into my hand and sliced out their big, oily livers. Getting them into Star wasn't going to be easy, but she was incapacitated, and I was a very powerful Apprentice. I would manage, but it wouldn't be pretty.

Grabbing her by the hair, I pulled Star's head back and crowded Naiadae and Zephrae into her mouth, opening her throat. Then I literally started pushing liver down into her with my fingers. By the time I managed to get that first liver past her gagging and writhing, she'd come around enough to push me away. Then she vomited. I had the other liver in my hand. Star saw it and started crying, which caused tears to well in my eyes. But I got myself together and said, "You *have* to eat it, or I'll have to do it again. *Please*, Star! I can't lose you!"

Weeping, but with at least some awareness in her eyes, Star took the other liver and started eating, trying her best not to gag. When I saw she was managing it and coming around, I went back to the water to call another fish. As I did, I had to wipe tears from my eyes. I knew if she didn't keep eating it by herself, I'd have to force her again.

XI
Treed

It's funny, but as soon as I opened my eyes, I knew what had happened. I'd fallen off the lines over the forest, and was now hanging from my pack, high in the boughs of a fir tree. A limb had skewered through the bottom of my pack and come out the top, leaving me dangling precariously.

The sun had barely been up when I'd fallen. Now it was full-moon lit night. Had I been unconscious an entire day? Then I heard a humming sound, and saw a vaguely glowing light rising toward me from below. "You shouldn't sleep in trees when you have no wings," I heard a concerned voice say. Then I saw that it was Claireth, spun up to her three-foot size and buzzing toward me on her wings.

"I fell," I told her. "This tree caught me."

"I don't think so," she said. "Trees live in different time. We go much too fast for them to see us."

"Okay," I said, trying to adjust myself into a comfortable position. "I *landed* in this tree. Do you think you could fly me down out of here?"

Claireth giggled, a lovely sound, and said, "You're *much* too big! But I can spin you down if you give me permission."

"Will it hurt?" I asked.

"Oh, no!" she said, giggling again. "I could *never* hurt you. We've played at love—we're LoveLinked. Do I have your permission?"

"What the helluva," I said. "Yes, you do."

I felt myself slip out of my pack, and all of a sudden I couldn't tell if my head was spinning or if *all* of me was spinning. Anyway, I *spun*! The next thing I knew I was sitting in Claireth's palms, looking up into her now huge, pretty face. She was smiling. In a moment she fluttered us down and set me on the ground. "Make me big again," I squeaked.

"I'll spin you up a bit," she said with a giggle. "But the last time we loved, you were so much bigger than me! I want to see what that was like!"

Again, my head spun (though the other way, it seemed), then I was standing next to Claireth, who was now just a head or so taller than me. "And let's do something about those obscene clothes once and for all," she huffed.

After running one hand down her other arm, Claireth threw some kind of glittering dust all over me. In a moment, it sparked my clothes to ash. I was a little bit scared, now, but also a little bit you know what. "Will you make me my normal size after we play? Remember, you said you wouldn't hurt me."

"Have I hurt you?" she asked with a genuine look of concern.

"No," I told her.

"And I *shan't*" she said through a wicked smile. She was very big, and seriously had her way with me.

FireSprites don't sweat, it seems, but I was soaked. "You just float me up to the clouds!" I told Claireth through my panting.

"I *know*! I can feel it coming off of you!" she sighed.

Still a little concerned, I asked, "Will you make me my regular size now please?"

"Oh, but you're *so cute*!" Claireth pouted.

"It'll upset me if you don't," I told her.

"Really?" she asked. Then she placed her fingers on my forehead and her eyes went wide. "Oh, it *does*!" she said. "Would you not be upset if I made you my size exactly...just for a while? I *promise* I'll make you regular later, *okay*?" she pleaded.

"Can't you make yourself bigger?" I asked.

"I could, but I wouldn't be able to fly, or make dust, or *anything*," she pouted.

"Okay," I agreed. "Just as big as you for now. But I wish you hadn't burned up my clothes."

"*No* one wears those here," she told me very seriously. "It's obscene! Lucky for you I'm open-minded."

"I think you're a little horny, too," I smiled.

"If that means what I think it means, I'm more than a little." Then she touched her fingers to my head again and said, "You, too."

Suddenly I was spinning till I was exactly Claireth's size. "Let's try it like this!" she grinned. Then she took me back up to the clouds.

XII
Despair

I stood there with that third liver in my hands, amazed that Star looked so much better. Slowly, taking very small bites, she was managing to eat. "Would it help if I cook this one a bit?" I asked her.

"Yes," she said, her voice a little hoarse and gaggy. "Did you have your entire hand down my throat?" she croaked.

"Pretty much," I said, looking around for a stick to skewer that liver.

As soon as I had it on a shaft of driftwood, Star said, "I'll do it," and the liver burst into flames.

"How do you feel?" I asked.

"Other than you opening my throat like a barrel?"

"I'm sorry."

"You saved me," she said very softly. "And I'm well enough. But something is very wrong, Spearl, and something has changed. It's no longer draining me...but...but..." Then her face pinched into terrible sadness, and she began to cry. "She's gone, Spearl," she sobbed. "I can feel it. Kimikin has fallen out of World!"

XIII
In a Friendly Glow

After loving with my exact-same-size darling Claireth, we lay in the grass under the stars and glowed. My feelings were love and friendship and adoration and pure lust. "You have such a *lovely* feel," Claireth said. "I'm smothered in it," she sighed.

"You're so beautiful," I said, turning up on an elbow to look at her gently glowing face—her dimples and pert little nose. And her ears were ever-so-slightly pointed! She was the kind of cute that made you want to swallow her whole!

"Yours is a strange beauty," she said, "but it intoxicates me. Are all aneke'lementals like you?"

"There's only one other," I told her. "My mother, though my father has a bit of Fierae about him."

"Are the *humans* like you?"

"Pretty much," I said. Then I started thinking about Daddy again. And Mother. "I need to go home, Claireth. I'm scared. Something has been stalking me, maybe a fox, and..."

"Fox!" Claireth exclaimed. "Tell me about the fox. No, come here, let me see for myself." Claireth touched her fingers to my head and said, "Think of the fox." In just a moment, she pulled her fingers away and whispered, "That's no fox!"

"Then what..."

"What have you done to attract that one's attention?" Claireth said, interrupting me.

"That one *what*?" I asked, feeling a touch of fear.

"Stop that!" she insisted in a harsh whisper. "No fear! It's a terrible smell here, and will attract nothing good!"

"Great, so just scare me some more," I said. "Tell me about the gollam fox!"

"He's a luminous being—Luminae, some say. He's a devious prankster, not a nice Luminae at all. He has many names, none of which I'll utter. If he's looking for you, you must hide. But in here, you stick out like a berry-stained thumb! We must get you some wings and make you look more like a Sprite. Come, we'll go to ClanHome."

Claireth and I walked quite a distance, then she said, "We're here. Time to go down."

After another good spin, we were both dragonfly size. Ahead of us I could see many little lights twinkling and darting around. In just a few minutes, we walked into a wonderful, shimmering village—the ClanHome of the Fiereste.

Almost immediately, several FireSprites as beautiful as Claireth buzzed over to us. A couple of them were boys, but wore the beauty of girls. "What is it?" one of the boys said, indicating me.

"She's a HalfFierae girl," Claireth told him. "We're LoveLinked, so be nice to her or I'll be cross with you!"

"We'll be nice to her, Claireth," one of the girls said. "Let's play with her! Me first!"

"Not now!" Claireth said harshly. "She's being stalked...by a *fox!*"

That startled the FireSprites, and one of them squeaked, "*That* fox?"

"Yes, him!" Claireth told her. "Now go find the surgeons. Tell them we need wings!"

"Surgeons?" I said.

"You mustn't ask about this majick, Kimikin. It is very strong and secret. If Dakini or Fairae ever gained this knowledge, no good would come of it." To the other FireSprites, she said, "Shoo now! Find the surgeons!" Then she touched her fingers to my forehead and I fell away into oblivion.

Oblivion lifted off me like a pale veil rising. I was lying flat on my stomach on what seemed to be a bed of fluffy cotton. "She'll be fine. Help her up," I heard a mellifluous male voice say.

Claireth and another girl helped me off the cotton. My back, between my shoulders, felt tight and itchy. "She's uncomfortable," Claireth said, and somebody sprinkled something powdery on me. The itch and tightness vanished. Then muscles in my back I didn't know I had started twitching, and I could feel a breeze...from my *wings!*

"Oh, they work fine!" Claireth giggled. "Learn to use them and we can love in the air!"

"We removed the fear as best we could," the male who'd spoken before said. "But she must be careful. We may not have

40

gotten it all. If she's hiding from that one, fear won't serve her. Her kind get majick-starved, so we gave her the ability to absorb metals through her feet. Even when she learns to fly, she should walk some."

"She needs a glow, and a healthy shimmer about her skin," Claireth told him.

"She *has* a glow, but doesn't seem able to access it," he said. "Here, how's this?"

Some kind of dust flew at me again, and I felt the air around me quiver. Then I noticed my glittery body glowing like Claireth's. "You're a *lovely* FireSprite," she told me. *"So pretty!"* Then, to everyone else, she said, "Shoo now! Fierae girls don't like you to watch!"

They all flew off, and Claireth laid me down in the cotton.

"Do you live here in ClanHome?" I asked, my fingers twirling her pale, almost baby-fine hair.

"I have no home," she told me. "Though there's always a house for me when I'm here. I'm a Rover. We keep watch throughout the BorderRealm, though nothing has come across for ages. Until you, of course, but our LoveLink proves you're not an enemy." In a conspiratorial whisper, she added, " If you were, I'd have to report."

"So you must travel a lot," I said.

"I fly far and wide!" Claireth smiled.

"Do you think you could get me home?"

"I can take you anywhere, but you wouldn't *be* there," she told me. "Well, actually you *would* be there, but your World wouldn't. You're here now, and we aren't allowed to embrace the fire and cross to the outward light. We haven't left the inward for over a thousand years. You mustn't cross again. If he's stalking you, he'll feel it the moment you try. You'd better be a FireSprite, now. And we mustn't use your real name, though I'll see that cutie pie on you always," she said with a blush. "So what shall we call you?"

"I don't know," I said. "What's a good FireSprite name?"

"I've always thought Ellannah was lovely."

"I've always liked Jill," I said, smiling.

"I'll call you Jil, then, but if anyone asks, your name is Jilhannah."

"I still want to go home," I told her

41

"I will take you," Claireth said, "but it won't be there. You must promise not to try and cross if I take you."

"I don't understand all this, Claireth," I told her. "But I'll do whatever it takes to get home. So I don't think I should promise."

"I may have to stop you," she said with a strange, sad look.

"You said you'd never hurt me," I told her.

"Then I'll have to keep you here with love," she said softly with her lips to my ear.

XIV
Meeting the Old Tenant

I left Star on the beach for the short while it took me to return to that clearing and fetch our packs. I'd left everything when I fled with her. Gryn, of course, had followed me faithfully.

By the time I returned, the sun was well up. Star seemed better, less despondent over Kimikin. But she was pensive, brow furrowed, and seemed to be concentrating on something. "What is it?" I asked.

Relaxing a bit, she looked at me and said quietly, "She isn't dead, Spearl. I can almost feel her, as if she's half-in, half-out of her body."

"She knows better than to come out," I told her.

"I know, Spearl. It's the only thing you've ever forbidden, and I think that frightens her. But she's *not* in World."

"Where else is there?" I asked.

"We must speak to the Fierae."

"*You* aren't coming out either. And I'm not the only one who's forbidden *that*."

"I know," she told me. "You must do it. I'll build a good fire and cook you fish—flesh as well as liver—and feed you when you return. Find out where my baby is, Spearl," she said, her face pitifully pinched and wet with tears.

"*Our* baby," I told her. "And *nothing*, not in World or out of it, will keep me from finding her. I swear it by Blitz' blood!" I said, surprising myself with that oath.

In the distance, I heard a roll of thunder. "Well, that certainly got someone's attention," Star said, her eyes wide with surprise that I'd sworn so.

"Good," I told her, though I wasn't so sure about that. "Build your fire. I'll build a storm."

It gathered out over the sea, and began to spin. They don't usually do that in springtime, but this storm seemed inspired by my ill-considered swearing. "You've done it now!" Star told me, majicking her fire against the wind and rain. "Do it, then send them back out to sea! How can I cook in this weather?"

About a hundred meters away, I saw a stingy palm with a ground charge up in its fronds. I left my body in the sand, and raced over there. It was nice being out of the wind and rain. "She comes comes comes," the charge was chittering. I still have trouble getting used to the fact that "she from above" is not uncommon now.

"Hello there!" I shouted, trying to get his attention.

"Is coming is coming!" he continued, oblivious of me.

"Hey!" I roared.

The charge stopped chittering, and after a moment, said, "Thirest the Cogitator! *Please* join!"

"Look closely," I said, shaking off the residual stain of Thirest's body.

"Spearl!" the charge exclaimed. "Will the Great Lady Pearl and the Hero Spaul coalesce and visit? What a joining *that* would be!"

"I don't know," I said. "But that would certainly be helpful. Can you arrange it?"

"I am but a charge," he told me. "Perhaps, once joined, a shout might be answered. Now she comes comes comes!"

The ground charge reached out of his tree, sending color and light into the storm. Then down she came, igniting them into a single being in the throes of ecstasy. "Spearl! Come to us! We have never joined with your like! Give us that thrill!"

"Could you give a shout to Mother and Father, first? Once I've spoken to them, I promise I'll join." Actually, it was all I could do *not* to join with them then and there.

"Stand back, little Fierae human. One comes, though not whom you seek."

I stood back a good distance as a light-body coalesced and boiled out of the Fierae joining. I recognized him immediately. I'd left his body in the sand by Star's fire. "Hello, Spearl!" he said to me.

"Thirest!"

"Can't stay long," he managed to say. I could see him fighting not to return to the Fierae. "Your daughter is stolen from World, but she hides in the borderlands. The thousand years are almost up, and Luminae are venturing abroad. One of the Third stole her, and seeks her now, though we're unsure why."

44

"What...?" I tried to ask, but he was already leaving.

"Can't stay!" he roared. "Take gentle blue poison to cross!"

"How are Mother and Father?" I called.

"Mighty with the Fierae!" he shouted, disappearing back into that bolt of love.

"Join now!" the Fierae screamed. "You promised!"

I had, and I did.

I rarely joined with the Fierae, as I knew they'd forbidden Star to leave her body. Even *in* her body, the call of the Fierae was strong for her, having dwelled with them for so long.

This joining left me quite depleted, more, it seemed, than it ever had before. Perhaps Thirest's presence had something to do with it. For all I knew, he was joined with us as well.

"Do you know your eyes are glowing a bit?" Star told me as she fed me roast fish and liver.

"Father's did that sometimes," I said, my voice still weak. "Remember?"

"I remember just about everything," she smiled. "Some of it is a burden. What did the Fierae say?"

"Thirest," I said, my mouth full of fish. "Thirest came."

"Really!" Star said, her eyes wide. "Mother and Father?"

"No, but I'm assured they're mighty with the Fierae."

Star smiled. "So, tell me, where is Kimikin?" she asked, her smile disappearing.

"He said she's not in World."

"I *told* you!"

"He said she's been sent to the borderland by something that's stalking her. She's been 'stolen,' he said."

"That *fox!*" Star said, anger flashing in her eyes.

"Or maybe a *Luminae?*" I added.

"What *are* Luminae?" Star said. "Blitz was so cryptic on the subject, and I've never seen or heard of such things."

"He said the thousand years are over, or almost, and they are venturing abroad, whatever that means. He also said we could 'cross,' I guess to the 'borderland,' by taking gentle blue poison. Mean anything?"

"Blue poison comes from the very type of sybic mushroom we found in that clearing! It's an alkaline psychotropic. Not sure

45

I've ever heard it called *gentle* blue poison, but I could see it being called that. It won't kill you."

"Isn't that something the first Starshine put in her potion to keep Mother on her sea?"

"Yes. But I don't see how that will take us anywhere, except out of our heads for a while. It's hallucinogenic."

"Sounds like fun," I smiled.

"It can be, but it doesn't mix well with fear, even a little bit. Not for the weak minded."

"Well, *I'm* not weak minded," I told her.

"Are you saying I am?"

"No, but you've been under a lot of stress. Maybe I should try this thing first, and you can watch over me. Baby-sit, so to speak."

I was very surprised when Star agreed to this. I was sure she would argue. "In the morning we'll go back to that clearing. I will 'baby-sit' you. But I honestly don't see this working. You're just going to get high as a kite and babble about lights and visions and similarly inane things. Will you be strong enough for this after just having joined?"

"If you keep feeding me, and hold me while I get a good sleep," I smiled.

"I can do both those things, my *other* baby."

XV
Teaching each other to Fly

I'd stopped blocking Mother the moment I dropped onto those lines that threw me. Now, as I walked with Claireth, I hoped she was aware of me. Thus far, I couldn't feel her touching my thought, and I'd always been able to whenever she did.

"Shall I teach you to use your wings?" Claireth asked.

"Didn't the *surgeon* say I should walk?" I said.

"Are you majick-starved?" she asked, concern drawing her mouth into a tight line.

"I don't think so," I told her.

"I don't mind walking," Claireth smiled. "But flying is *fun*, and *fast*!"

"If I take off on these wings, you'll want to love me up there!" I said, her beauty starting to melt me again.

"Of *course*!" she said, matter-of-factly.

"You know," I told her, 'I could take us both up high with*out* flying."

"How?" she asked, skeptically.

"Fold back your wings and I'll show you."

When both of us had our wings tight against our bodies, I called a chorus of Zephs and cocooned us. As we rose, Claireth said excitedly, "You're a witch! A wonderful, wonderful witch!"

"Apprentice," I told her. "And aneke'lemental."

"Can you do many tricks," she asked with a delighted smile.

"Yes," I told her.

"Oh! But you *shouldn't*," she said, her face suddenly gone all anxious. "He'll feel this majick! It isn't from here!"

"This trick is already done," I told her. "Wouldn't you like to play while we float like this?"

"It's *you* that's the hornedly one," she said, smiling.

"Horny," I smiled back. "You just make me that way."

"Ooooooooh!" she cooed.

When we were back on the ground, Claireth made me promise not to use my majick anymore, lest *he* find me. "I'd just grieve *forever* if something happened to you!" she told me. "Now let's unfold our wings and teach you to fly!"

I wasn't a very good pupil. Even after Claireth explained and coached and encouraged and promised erotic incentives, all I could do was stand there and buzz my wings furiously—kicking up dust, but not my feet off the ground. "Oh! You're trying too hard!" she finally said. "Relax!" Then she wiped dust from all over her body and threw it at me. "There," she said. "Now just *flutter*! Don't buzz."

Her dust make me feel light. I slowed my thrumming wings and suddenly my feet lifted several inches off the ground. I also managed to move backward and forward a bit. "It's a start," Claireth told me. "But we shan't tangle in FlutterLove quite yet."

"Mmmm, what's that?" I asked.

"*Learn*, and you'll find out!" she grinned.

Though Claireth and I were walking downhill, and I *seemed* to recognize our surroundings as the way I came, it was night here, and it seemed to be never ending. "How long till dawn?" I asked.

"I don't know, we're not there," she told me. "I've never seen it."

"Never seen the sun?"

"You don't pay attention, Cutie Pie," she smiled. "We haven't been allowed in the outward light for a very long time."

"So it's always night?" I asked.

"Always *inward*," she answered. "Watch the sky. It changes. Soon you'll see the Inward Light pass through it. When it rises, we call that *drawn*. We call the time it is in the sky, *summon*. Now, it is *not* in the sky, and we call this time *night*," she said with a grin. "It won't be long. As drawn nears you will see it drinking from the stars. In *that* world, light arrives. In *this* one, it departs. That's why our majick is so powerful. Yours is also wicked strong here. I felt it when you floated us."

Though I wasn't sure about what she was telling me, my majick *had* felt different to me. Easier. Performed with no effort. "When you say, *that* world, you mean *my* world, don't you?" I asked.

"I want *this* to be your world now, *Jilhannah*," she smiled, though a little sadly. "Our LoveLink is strong. And you're *such* a lovely FireSprite. They even pointed your ears a tiny bit. Wouldn't you like to stay with me?"

48

"Of course I would," I told her. "But I don't know what the Universe intends. I can only hope."

"I *very much* hope," Claireth said with love shimmering on her face.

"Don't let me miss the drawn," I said, looking up at the stars, which seemed very much like part of *my* world. "Does the moon ever rise?"

"It is there," Claireth answered. "But it has no light of its own."

XVI
Not so Gently Blue

I woke before dawn, but I curled tighter into Star's caressing arms. Then she whispered in my ear, "Liver for breakfast?" I moaned.

Once we'd eaten, tidied our packs, and were ready to head back inland, Star and I stood for an uncomfortable minute saying nothing. Then she raised her eyebrows, smiled at me and said, "Lines?"

I'd hoped Star would have the strength to call them, but wondered if it might take both of us, in our depleted states, working together to be able to ride. "I..." I said, which wasn't much help.

"Can't," she finished for me. It would be a good day before I could do much of anything, and she knew it.

"I can *see* them," I told her.

"And you intend to swallow psybic mushrooms and try to 'cross' to the 'borderland'?" Then she called up strong lines running to the west, and I felt the tingle of her powerfully charging my hands.

"You seem pretty well recovered." I said. Considering the dangerous condition she'd been in just hours before, this recovery seemed incredible.

"I'm aneke'lemental, Spearl. Remember? Whatever was assaulting me has ceased, but I might not have survived it without you. It was a very powerful phenomenon. It felt like something thirsty drinking my life and light."

I felt a little helpless, especially considering that blood oath I'd sworn. "I'll eat more liver," I said, lamely.

"I didn't argue when the situation was reversed," Star told me when we arrived back at the mushroom clearing. "And you mustn't argue now!"

"You *knew* this would happen when you sent me to the Fierae! You planned it all along," I argued.

Star showed me a sad little smile, and said in a hushed, tired voice, "Plotting traces." Then her tone became stern and she said, "Nothing is hindering me, Spearl! I'm well and totally able. You'll be majick-starved at least the rest of the day, even if I shoved liver down *your* throat."

"Then we wait!" I told her.

I was sitting against the sycamore where Star said Kimikin had slept. Suddenly I realized I was tied securely to it with Star's majick. Her Terrae held me fast. "Don't do this!" I warned. Then I begged, "*Please* don't do this, Star!"

"In all things, I've tried to defer to you, Spearl. You were wise even when we were children. But if the blue of these mushrooms will take me to my daughter—and I still have my doubts—I'm going. My Terrae will release you when I'm gone, but if you try to follow, try to swallow any mushrooms, they'll stop you and tie you again. One of us must watch, keep their wits."

"Will you be able to neutralize the poison if this goes wrong?" I asked, resigned now to the inevitable.

Star didn't answer, but started picking mushrooms and putting them into her mouth. Finally, having eaten at least six, she said, "No." Then she picked and ate four more.

Star came and sat leaning against me. Her Terrae released my arms, and I held her. "Can you feel it?" I asked.

"If they work according to their properties, I should feel a strong rush of energy, as if I'd taken strong stimulants. Then that will settle, and my mind will fold into hallucination. Hold me tight when the rushing begins, I took a lot. You'll feel my muscles tense."

Not a minute after she said that, Star's muscles *relaxed completely,* and I realized she was asleep. She felt somehow...I don't know...*thin* to me. She stayed deeply asleep for perhaps five minutes, then suddenly she was gone. As quickly as she vanished she was back in my arms, her eyes fluttering open and squinting in the morning light.

XVII
A Little Bit Crossed

Claireth and I walked together in silence a while, both of us, I think, a bit awed by our growing love. Then she said to me, "Look, drawn is upon us."

Just as she said that, we arrived at a round clearing. I looked up and saw streamers coming off the stars nearest the eastern horizon. They seemed to be bleeding light toward the "drawn." It was beautiful, but something diverted my attention. "This is the clearing where I first saw you!" I told Claireth.

Touching her fingers to my forehead, she smiled and said, "And you dreamed of me after, didn't you?"

I blushed. Then I looked back to the sky and saw a dark disc through the treetops. It looked like the sun (which most call the Ball) surrounded by rays of dark blue light that seemed to be radiating *in* instead of *out*. "The Inward Light," Claireth said, seeing my fascination. Then she looked into the clearing toward the sycamore I'd slept against. "*Another* one?" she said. "If this keeps up, I'll *have* to report!"

"Another what?" I asked.

"One like *you*. Can't you see her?"

"*Her?*" I exclaimed. Could it be Mother? "I don't see her!"

Claireth placed her fingers on my forehead and said, "Be still and look."

There she was—thin, like a ghost. "Mother!" I called out, and she vanished.

"You don't *listen*, Cutie Pie! Be *still!*" Claireth scolded.

I quieted, felt those delicate fingers on my brow, then saw Mother again. Her eyes were wide and she was saying something, but no words came.

"Stay still," Claireth reminded. "Can you hear what she says?"

"No," I whispered.

"She says she loves you, she's sorry, and is...*thrilled*...by your lovely new beauty."

"I don't think she said that last part," I told her.

"I paraphrased," Claireth smiled. "She is only half crossed. Her majick is different than yours, not so strong in certain respects. When you cross, your light-body changes to accommodate this inward nature. She clings to her outward light-body. It resists changing to allow her to cross."

Suddenly, Mother's eyes and look grew determined. It seemed she was pulling against something that was holding her back. Then, with a little popping sound, she became solid and said, "We're rescuing you! Your father is here!"

"I've been trying to come home!" I told her as she rushed forward to embrace me. But just as we met, she disappeared.

"She needs practice," Claireth told me matter-of-factly. "She must exercise her majick if she wants to cross and stay put. But if she *does* come again, I'm going to be *forced* to report!"

"Report to who?" I yelled at her, frustrated with being so close and then losing Mother.

I immediately wished I hadn't yelled. Claireth's beautiful face fell to pitiful crying. Her perfect tears sparked when they hit the ground. "I don't know," she wept. "It's been so long since any have crossed, we've forgotten who we report to."

For a long while I kissed away Claireth's tears, which fizzled on my lips. She seemed even more distraught about not being able to report than I was about Mother. "I'm sorry," I whispered again and again. "I shouldn't have yelled at you."

"I *know*!" she sobbed. "Our LoveLink is *strong*. You could have *hurt* me. But mostly I'm upset about the reporting. I should have told you the truth."

"Don't be silly, it was none of my business," I told her. "And I don't *ever* want to hurt you."

All of a sudden, Claireth's tears stopped, and an anxious look stole her face. "We need to hide!" she said. "That was very strange majick. He'll *certainly* feel it!"

In a flash, I was spinning until Claireth and I were firefly size. "You're light as a feather now, and must fly! We need to get away from here." Taking me by the hand, she said, *"Flutter!"*

In an instant we were both airborne. "You're okay with up and down," she told me, "but you can't *go* yet, can you?"

"Not really," I told her.

53

"Don't worry, I'll pull you! I like holding your hand, anyway."

"Me, too," I said. "Pull me east. Let's find the Ninety-five and head for home."

"It won't be there, Cutie Pie," Claireth reminded me.

"But it's where I told Mother I was going. And I have a *feeling*. A lot of majick has dwelled there over the years."

Claireth furrowed her brow for a moment, then said, "Residual majick is weak, though it *does* accumulate. I suppose it *is* possible, my smart little Cutie Pie."

When we found the Ninety-five, Claireth stopped us and said softly, with a look in her eyes that made me go gooey, "Just flutter, now. Flutter, my love."

XVIII
Despondent

As soon as Star's eyes blinked open, she began to cry. "Hold me tightly," she said, closing her eyes again. "The blue is still with me. I'm lost in a whirl of color!"

What she said next made little sense, and I took it to be the ramblings of the drug. She was saying Kimikin had changed, was a "Fairae" now, and was somehow joined to another such creature. "I tried I tried I tried," she sobbed. "So close so close, her skin powdered with sparkle sparkling she's naked and glowing, my poor poor baby!"

For hours I held her as she'd rant, then go calm, then rant again. Finally she slept, though her muscles twitched as if lectrics ran through her. Eventually, I slept as well.

XIX
A Possible Development

FlutterLove. How can I describe it? Apparently the muscles that power my wings never tire. Together, Claireth and I performed a wonderful dance of love in the sweet, sweet air. And our *wings*! When our wings caressed, like butterflies kissing, the ecstasy was nearly explosive! It seemed to last for hours, and our skin, our fingers, our tongues, grew *hot*! Claireth's dust poured from her and enveloped us in a glittering cloud that sparked and sizzled around us, over us, into us! I didn't think it would ever end until Claireth held me away by the shoulders and said, in a quivery voice, "We must stop, now. Our light is beginning to mingle. If we keep on, one, or *both*, may spark a babe."

I could barely hear her—was trying desperately to embrace her again, to get my hands on her, my tongue on her.

"Can you hear me, Cutie Pie?" she smiled, holding me back. "Are you ready to have a baby?"

Somehow, I controlled myself and we fluttered down into what was for us a forest of grass. "Baby?" I said, my breath still hot and coming in gasps. "How could *we* have a baby? Don't you need a boy for that?"

"That's a much *different* way," she giggled, "but not a *need*. And it's *messy*, unless you're inclined to that sort of love."

"I'm not," I said.

"Me, neither," she whispered. "Though I've tried it just to see."

"What's it like?" I asked her.

"Messy," she said, scrinching her pretty little nose.

"But you and I could..."

"*Would* have, had I not stopped us. I think you'd have been first, but if we mingled long enough, I would have, too."

"Would have..?" I asked.

"*Conceived*, you goose! What did you think I was talking about?"

"I'm not sure," I muttered, trying to take it all in. Then I smiled said, "But I think my mother may like you. *Now*, will you love me like that again, please?"

"Too soon," she smiled. "We'd be right back where we left off in an instant. Do you *want* me to spark you a babe?" she said, her smile gone and her look very serious.

"Not today," I told her.

"'Tis not a thing to do lightly," she frowned.

"If at all," I said.

For a moment, Claireth seemed a touch saddened. But it disappeared immediately, and she said, resolutely, "Yes! One must be absolutely certain, or not allow it at all!"

We lay in that grass forest for some time, holding one another and occasionally quivering with the memory of that play. "It takes a while to settle such a love," Claireth told me.

"You're not helping," I said, which made her giggle.

"Up now," she told me. "My dust has stopped pouring, and the wet you shed has dried on your skin. Shall we continue our journey?"

I was about to say yes and then steal a kiss, when I heard buzzing overhead, and someone say, "What have we here? FireSprite Rovers tangled in play?"

"Fairae!" Claireth said to me. "Just try to ignore them."

Two girls fluttered down next to us, who looked *very* much like FireSprites to me. If anything, perhaps they didn't glow quite as much. Then one of them spoke again, looking right at me. "Wait!" she said. "This one looks more Dakini! Been slumming, Claireth?"

"She's a *FireSprite!*" Claireth said in a dangerously angry voice. "She's just a little love-drained."

"And *you!*" the other Fairae said, looking Claireth up and down. "You're *LoveLocked* aren't you? And when she's finished with you, you'll be Love *Torn!*"

As the Fairae giggled, Claireth's anger vanished, and I thought I saw her chin quiver. I can't *tell* you how much that affected me! So much so that I walked over and pushed that Fairae girl, knocking her down. "*I'm* the one LoveLocked," I told her. "And if you make my darling cutie pie cry, I'll pull off your wings!"

I must have looked pretty fierce, because the two Fairae buzzed and took off. From a safe distance, they taunted us once more, singing, "Oh Cutie Pie! Oh Cutie Pie! I'll love you till the stars all die!" Then they laughed and flew away.

Claireth had the strangest look on her face, and I couldn't tell if she was going to smile or cry. "Are you?" she finally said in a tiny voice.

"What?" I asked, taking her into my arms.

"LoveLocked?" she whispered in my ear.

"I might be," I whispered back.

"Me, too," she said, gently weeping.

XX
Tool's Warning

Day was nearly done when Star and I woke in that clearing. "Are you alright?" I asked, holding her tightly.

"I saw her, Spearl. I was there for an instant. She's changed. She has wings and is small and glowing."

"I think the drug still has you," I said.

"It's gone. When it subsided enough, I neutralized it. Our daughter is...*something*. Something out of myth! But she said she was trying to get home. We have to go! It's a different world, Spearl, I saw it, *felt* it. Always night and full of majick wanting to fly. Strong, strong majick that has changed our baby. But she's still beautiful. *So beautiful!*" she said, her eyes losing focus. "If she wasn't our poor baby I'd marvel at that beauty. But I want her back the way she was! I want her *human!*"

"She was never human, Star, and neither were you."

"But we *look* human, Spearl. Kimikin doesn't look human anymore." Then she wept again and I held her tighter.

"Get your strength back," I told her. "*Both* of us need our strength back. We should eat and then sleep again. In the morning, once we're recovered, we'll be able to fly home in a flash. If that's where she's going, we'll get her back. By..."

But Star put her fingers on my lips and said, "No more oaths, Spearl. You'll bind yourself to them."

"I'm bound to that purpose," I told her, and I was.

Next morning, I was well and could call lines. Star was also recovered, and picking mushrooms. "We'll need these," she said, stuffing them into her pack. "I'll distill them into a powerful draught."

"They made a mess of you." I told her.

"But they got me there," she countered. "I need to cogitate on what happened, Spearl. I need to define this majick. There is another world, and there is a way to cross into it. Kimikin is proof, and Thirest hinted at how."

"It was a brief conversation," I told her. "He could have been more specific."

"He's been with the Fierae a very long time, Spearl. It must have taken all his will to stay as long as he did. Together, we'll figure it out. Now let's go. I've enough mushrooms here to sauce the minds of everyone in Ginny."

Star flew us home even faster than I'd flown her majick-starved body to the beach. Immediately, she started boiling those mushrooms. The water in her pot was turning a toxic blue. "I'm going out to the barn for a minute," I told her.

"Bring a jug in," she said. "I could use a little bracer myself."

With a small jug of Corn in my hand, I plopped down onto a haystack in the barn. Then I turned up the jug and swallowed more than a little bracer. "You sure knew how to make Corn, Grandfather," I said out loud, and I could hear him saying when I was in my young, other body, "It *strong*, Spearl. Don't take too much."

I was about to take another pull, when I heard him again, but this time it didn't seem to be in my head. "Too strong, Spearl. She takin' too much."

I shivered once, and tears filled my eyes. Then I looked up and said, "Thank you, Grandfather!"

Still holding the jug, I ran to the house. Bursting in, I startled Star. "What is it?" she said.

"Too *much!*" I told her. "You took too much. It takes only a little bit—*gentle* blue poison—to help you cross!"

Star closed her eyes, and I could see she was cogitating. Finally, she opened them and smiled. "How did you figure it out? I don't think I'd have ever seen it!"

I smiled back, handed her the jug and said, "Just remember what Grandfather told you about Corn."

"It's a neke'lemental majick you need in order to cross," Star told me, after a tiny sip of Corn, "facilitated by a touch of blue poison. I took so much back at the clearing that it affected my light-body. It was holding it here, keeping it from changing into what it must be in that world."

"So it's complicated," I said, smiling and taking the jug from her.

"Not too much of that, now. You'll need to neutralize it before we make our attempt."

"I'm still good," I told her, taking another sip.

"I've heard that before," she said. "Be *careful!*"

"So when do we do this?"

"Tomorrow, I think. As best I can cogitate, it would be good to try it at dawn...or perhaps dusk. We *could* try it now, but I'd like to consider it further. I also want to cool and bottle my blue poison extract."

"I thought we'd only need a little."

"We will, but if I'm right, we'll need a little to get back, and so will Kimikin. She's here, Spearl. I know it! She's here in another world."

XXI
Home in Another World

It's amazing how fast tiny FireSprites can fly. Faster, even, than traveling the lines, and *much* faster than spun-up-to-three-feet-size FireSprites can go. *Our* speed, however, was hampered by my arm, which threatened to pull out of the socket if Claireth pulled me along too quickly. Several times, we stopped for a "lesson."

"Fly up with me *high*," Claireth told me.

"What are we going to do?" I asked.

"It's a *lesson*, Cutie Pie! Just do as I say, and don't worry so much. You must know by now that I'd die before I allowed you to come to harm."

When she said that, I absolutely believed her, and to tell the truth, it scared me a little. Not how she *felt* about me, but the thought of her dying. It caught in my throat and misted my eyes. "Come on!" she said, rocketing straight up.

I followed her, but I wasn't as fast. Finally, we were both hovering way, way high. "Now fold your wings back and dive! Don't worry, they'll open by themselves, and when they do, soar toward the direction you want. It's a *different* way to go. You'll find it easier."

I did trust her, and followed her instructions. As soon as I folded my wings, I dove headlong and fast toward *down*! Then I spread my wings, maneuvered myself to fly south, and I *soared*! What a feeling! Then I heard Claireth beside me, laughing. "You're *wonderful*!" she shouted.

"I wish you could love me like this!" I shouted back.

For a moment her eyes went wide, then Claireth said, "I'll have to think about it, but if there's a way!" Then she zoomed in circles around and over and under me. "You're a *magnificent* FireSprite, Cutie Pie!" she cried.

Soaring and fluttering, walking and running, kissing and giggling, Claireth and I finally made it to where home should have been. Though there was no house or barn, it looked very familiar. "There's a pond over that ridge," I told Claireth. "The barn is here, and the house over there."

"Not here," she told me.

"Why do you keep saying things like that?" I asked her.

"Oh, I'd *never* lie to you, or let you lie to yourself!" she told me, and I could see pure love in her eyes as she said it. So I kissed her. And she kissed me back.

"What do you think we should do now?" I asked.

"I don't know," she said. "What had you intended to do?"

"Try to get back, I guess," I told her.

"You *are* back. They're the ones in a different world."

"But I'm not *supposed* to be in this world," I said.

"How," she said, hands on her hips, "can you *not* be supposed to be here when you *are* here? Do you hear yourself?"

I had to laugh. "Please don't confuse me more than I already am," I said. "Let's just wait and see what happens."

"Let's swim in the pond!" Claireth squealed. "I may not know how to love you soaring, but I could *boil* you in a pond!" There was simply no way to say no to that.

Swimming was lovely! When Claireth got into the water, the whole pond lit up. Glittering dust floated everywhere, and at one point, we were nearly like we were when we FlutterLoved. "Now, now!" Claireth warned. "If sparks share, babes we'll bear!"

"Oh, it's so *hard*!" I said, backing away from her. "At some point I won't be able to stop, and there'll be babies *everywhere*!"

"Only once," she said.

"What do you mean?" I asked.

"The sparks will only fly once each. After that we could love till we melt, but it wouldn't happen again."

"Maybe we should get it over with!" I laughed.

"Not a good reason to spark a babe. You know better," she scolded.

"I was *kidding*!" I smiled. "*Sort*-of."

"Out, now, enough!" Claireth told me.

"No, wait," I said. "You stay in, I have a surprise for you."

I climbed out of the pond and sat on the bank. Then I spoke to the Naiadae surrounding Claireth. "Oh!" she squeaked.

"Relax," I told her.

I played my Naiadae over Claireth's gorgeous little body until the pond began to *shine*! She squealed and moaned and sighed and screamed! Finally, she floated onto her back and said in a pitiful voice, "Oh, *please*!"

I waded in and carried her out of the pond. "You mustn't *do* that to me," she gasped. Then she sighed again and said, "Unless I *beg* you to!"

We walked back over the ridge. Claireth, still love-weak and sighing, said, "Your majick is very nearly *naughty*, Cutie Pie. You found a way to take me where babes spark without letting it happen. Now I have to find a way to do it to *you*!"

"If there's anything I can do to help," I smiled.

She thought about that for a minute, then said, "Teach me to speak to the Naiadae!"

"I just gave you quite a lesson," I grinned.

"But I couldn't pay attention!" she said very seriously. "I was liquefying!"

I laughed, which caused her to laugh, and we came up over the ridge laughing. Then I stopped, looked at her and said, "Did you hear something?"

"Us laughing?" she asked.

"No. I think I heard Mother touch my thought."

XXII
Crossed

"I heard her laughing, Spearl! For just an instant, I could feel her!"

"That's it, let's go!" I said. "What do we do?"

"Let's go into the yard," she told me, grabbing up her jar of blue poison.

Once we were out there, we stood face to face and each dipped a finger into the blue. Then we stuck those fingers in each other's mouths. "Do you feel it, Spearl?" Star asked me.

"I feel dizzy."

"Let yourself go. It's a bit like falling. Feel your light-body wanting to change. Let it!"

It was just dawn when we put blue fingers into our mouths. Suddenly, the stars seemed to melt toward the eastern horizon. Then I heard laughing and saw two children, naked and winged, running down from the ridge. Suddenly, one of them fluttered her wings and flew into my arms. "Daddy!"

XXIII
In the Light

After kisses and hugs and tears and apologies, I said, "Daddy, Mother, this is Claireth."

"You're so *beautiful!*" Mother told her.

"I'm very happy to meet you," Claireth said. "But I have to admonish you—wearing those clothes in front of your daughter! Aren't you embarrassed?"

"And *she* has an open mind," I smiled, hugging Claireth to me.

"We're not staying," Mother said. "We've come to take Kimikin home."

"Hush!" Claireth scolded. "Don't say her real name. He'll hear! She is Jilhannah, now, of the Clan Fiereste!"

"Who will hear?" Mother asked.

"The fox," I told her.

"Hush!" Claireth said again.

Mother turned to Daddy and said, "Let's go, Spearl—same trick in reverse. Come on, Kimikin, I'll show you how."

"Jilhannah!" Claireth insisted.

"I don't know, Mother," I said.

"Don't know *what?*"

"I can't leave Claireth. We're LoveLinked at *least*, and maybe more! It's very serious. And, anyway, look at me. This is strong majick and, I think, permanent!"

"I'll find a way..." she began, but Daddy stopped her.

"I don't think you will," he said. "Look at the anatomy of her wings, the musculature. It's all normal and natural, Star. You'll never change it."

"I don't care!" Mother cried, tears falling from her eyes. "Come home, Kimikin! Please! Bring Claireth with you. I'll be happy for your love, I promise! I don't *care* if the aneke'lemental line ends!"

"It *might* not," I said, smiling wickedly at Claireth, who was smiling wickedly at me. "We're FireSprites, Mother, and our love can spark a babe."

"Two!" Claireth chirped.

"Please come with us, Claireth," Mother begged. "We can't stay here."

"Not in those obscene clothes!" Claireth told her.

"My majick isn't strong enough to stay," Mother said. "I can already feel World pulling me back."

I looked over at Daddy, and he suddenly became a ghost. Then he disappeared. "Quickly, you two!" Mother cried, holding out a jar of something blue. "Dip a finger in and put it in your mouth. You'll feel it, Kimikin! You'll know what to do!"

She was pleading, begging me, holding that jar out to me as she started to fade away. Quickly, I snatched it out of her hand, and she was gone. I was alone again with Claireth. "I have to go to them," I told her, sticking my finger into the jar.

"I can't part from you," Claireth said, putting hers in as well. Then we sucked on each other's fingers, and fell out into the light.

"Ouch!" was the first thing Claireth said as we found ourselves standing in bright morning light, out in the yard of my home.

"What's wrong?" I asked her.

"This outward light burns!" she cried.

"Get her into the house, Kimikin," Mother was saying. "Quickly, before she's red as a beet!"

Taking Claireth by the hand, I led her up onto the porch and into the morning coolness in the house. "I didn't know the Ball would burn you so," I told her, taking her in my arms and giving her a kiss.

"Does it not burn *you*?" she asked.

"Sometimes, if I stay out in it too long. But not as quickly as it was burning you. I guess I'm more used to it."

"I'll not get used to burning," Claireth said, her pretty chin quivering and tears misting her eyes. "Maybe we should go back."

"But we just got here!" I told her. "Don't you want to see my world?" Then I whispered in her little pointed ear, "We can love here as well, you know. Something new to try?"

My enticements didn't seem to do much to mollify Claireth, and then Mother and Daddy came through the door. They seemed at a loss for words. Finally, Mother said, "Let me find you something to wear."

Claireth's eyes grew wide, and she said to me in a harsh whisper, "She doesn't mean *clothing*, does she? Because there'll be absolutely none of *that*! I'll not play lewd games, especially with total strangers. *Perhaps...* for *you*...in *private*...I might...I might..." Though Claireth didn't glow in our world, her blush certainly did as she whispered in my ear, "...I *might* let you dress me."

Claireth and I had gone to my room. I told Mother and Daddy we needed to rest, but I really wanted to shelter Claireth a bit, as she wasn't exactly taking a shine to our world. I think, to her, it all seemed brassy and crass. And though her social mores might seem outrageous here, she was actually a bit parochial—at least within the confines of her "normal" conventions.

So I drew the curtains in my room tight against the sun, and introduced Claireth to my bed. Putting one of my pillows to her face, she said, "It smells of you...not an *entirely* unpleasant odor."

"I don't stink," I told her.

"This whole world smells funny, Jilhannah."

"You can call me Kimikin again," I told her. "Mother and Daddy will protect us here. Nothing can harm us."

Claireth smiled and said, "I love seeing your name on you, and *hearing* it melts me. But I'm not so sure how safe you are if he's still looking for you."

"Let's not think about that now," I said, touching my lips to hers. Then, after a quick knock, my door opened. "Mother!" I whined.

"I'm sorry," she said, averting her eyes, which for some reason made me giggle. "I found these robes from when you were younger, Kimikin. I think they'll fit if you can...if your wings will..."

"We'll manage, Mother. Now we're trying to *rest*."

"Let me know if you get hungry," she said in an embarrassed voice as she left the room. I got up and locked it behind her. "As if locks will keep her out," I muttered to myself. Then I turned back to Claireth, who seemed to have gone all shy. She looked so pretty, so *vulnerable*. And I'm sure my grin must have been wicked as I went to my dresser and pulled out a skimpy little blouse. Then I walked over to Claireth, sitting in the bed, and said, "Come here, you darling cutie pie. Fold back you wings and let me put this on you."

"Oh!" Claireth chirped, and I could see the dust just pouring off of her.

XXIV
World Sick

Mother said Daddy had an errand to which he must attend. Even though I'd been blocking her furiously from touching my thought, I could read *her* like a book. She'd *sent* Daddy on some errand, and it had to do with *me*!

Claireth was sleeping a lot, something I'd never seen her do in her world. She could not come out into daylight without burning, and absolutely refused to wear the little, hooded robe Mother made for her—at least not out of my room. "I'll wear it *here*, for *you*," she told me. "But I'll not go about like that for everyone to see. I'm not some floozy Dakini temptress, you know. I'm a FireSprite of the Clan Fiereste, and a Rover!"

At night Claireth did come alive. We played in the pond, and even flew a tiny bit, though it was hard for us both, and especially Claireth. She always complained of being *heavy*. "And I can't *spin* here," she told me. "We're stuck this size, which worries me if there should come a time when we need to hide."

"Let me show you something," I told her one night when she was fretting terribly. We'd just come out of the pond, and our love had been less than enthusiastic. "You're worried again, aren't you?" I asked her. She said nothing, and I told her, "Watch!"

When my eyes and skin began to glow, she cooed, "Oh! That's *lovely*!"

Then I released a white stream of fire, and turned a small cedar into a blazing torch. "Oh, my!" Claireth yelped.

Once I'd settled myself, though I was still pretty warm to the touch, I took her in my arms and said, "I won't let anything harm you, and neither would Mother or Daddy. We're very strong, and there isn't much in this world that can threaten us."

"When he comes," she whispered, "he'll come from *that* world."

"But then he'll be in *this* one," I told her, "and he'd better behave."

Together, Claireth and I were becoming pretty much nocturnal creatures. But one morning, after she'd fallen deeply asleep, I felt hungry and ventured out to the kitchen. Mother was sitting there, having just gotten up, drinking tea. "Anything to eat?" I asked her.

"Won't you at least wear a robe in broad daylight?" she said to me. "Especially when your father gets back. Doesn't it bother you to be naked around him?"

"I don't even think about it, Mother," I said. "FireSprites see clothes as naughty, if not obscene."

"You're not a FireSprite, Kimikin."

"Take a good look, Mother. I'm three feet tall, with wings and little pointed ears."

"I think you could change that, Kimi...change yourself back."

Her calling me Kimi didn't score any points, and I was getting angry. "You've *always* wanted to change me, Mother! And *this*," I said, running the backs of my hands down my body, "for your trouble, is what I've changed into. What I love the very most, more than you can imagine, is *like* me, and likes me very much the way I am. I may even ask her to give me a child. Isn't that what you've always wanted, Mother, a grandbaby to play with? Will you shun her if she has little wings?"

I started to storm out of there, but Mother said, "Kimikin! Wait! Will Claireth not love you if you become a human girl again?"

"I was *never* a human girl, Mother," I said, walking away. "I can't believe you'd even suggest it!"

Between Claireth's growing anxiety, and Mother's determination to change me back, I was becoming a bit unnerved. The love Claireth and I played was less and less ...*volatile*, and I found myself getting, on occasion, a little short with her. "How will we ever spark a babe like this?" I said to her one night out by the pond. The moon was huge and full, and Claireth seemed unable to take her eyes off it.

"We'll not spark a babe here," she whispered, still looking up into that pale light.

"What do you mean?" I asked her.

"Even if we could, somehow, love to such heights in this place, I'd be loathe to bring a babe here."

What she said made me sad, but also determined to restore our love. "Come with me," I said, leading her into the pond.

As I played gentle kisses on her lips, I roused my Naiadae. "Oh, my!" Claireth yelped.

After a good bit of that, the water around us parted as I cocooned us in Zephrae and floated us up toward that moon. Our love became so frantic it roused my fire, and I became hot to the touch. It lasted a very long time, until finally we found ourselves back on the ground, spent and lying in the cool grass. I was holding Claireth close, gently singing to her. Then I touched my hand to her belly and said in a tiny whisper, "Is there a baby in here?"

"No," she whispered back, and I could tell she was weeping. Then she placed her hand on my stomach and said in a sad, sad voice, "But there may be one here."

XXV
Errand of Lunacy

Star had convinced me to go seek the help of one of the more talented New Apprentices. Wanda May, she was called, and she lived due west of us up in the foothills. I'd have preferred it if Star had gone, but she insisted on staying to protect "the girls."

Though they were definitely female, and exhibited it constantly, I had trouble thinking of them as "girls." Girls were human, for the most part, but my daughter and her lover were something else.

Wanda May, Star seemed to believe, had some higher understanding of the Linea Clipses. She was convinced she could help me use Gryn to change Kimikin. I doubted it, and was hesitant to use *any* majick that involved those lines to the moon.

There were some places between us and Wanda May where I simply could not travel on the lines. Star is probably the only one in World who can ride over heavy forest, though Kimikin, I think, has that potential.

It was four days later that I finally came back over the ridge and could see my home. It had been a fool's errand. Mostly I succeeded only in scaring the wits out of Wanda May when I used Gryn to call the Linea Clipses into the night sky. "I know *of* them," she told me. "But I'd never *seen*! I know you use Gryn to heal, but to change a person into a *different* person? You'd call down the moon and kill us all!"

It took a lot of promises to convince Wanda May that I would *not* try that majick. I ended up staying long enough to cure the chicken pox that was running though their little village. It was majick that only Gryn and I could perform. I left carrying bundles of food and my pack full of little gifts. There was a stuffed-toy muley that I would give to Kimi. And, believe it or not, a little carving of a "fairae" that would go to Claireth. Star was going to get a bit of ire.

It was early morning when I arrived at the house. I entered quietly. Immediately, I heard a ruckus in the kitchen. "So they changed you without so much as a *by your leave*, these *surgeons!*" Star said angrily.

"It wasn't like that, Mother. They were trying to *hide* me. They were very afraid for my safety! It just happened so *fast*. Claireth touched me unconscious and the next thing I knew..."

"So *she* did this! She remade you to her liking!"

Then I heard a *slap*, and Kimikin came storming through the kitchen door. There were tears in her eyes, and I could see she wanted to run into my arms. But she looked down at her glittery little body, cried out in despair, and ran to her room.

I walked into the kitchen where Star stood with her palm on a slapped-red cheek. "What *else* have you been saying to her besides what I heard?" I said, dangerous anger in my voice.

Star turned her back to me and said softly, "She needs to come back to us, Spearl. What did you find out from Wanda May?"

"Exactly what you probably knew I'd find. It can't be done. Did you send me there so you could torment our daughter? There is *no changing* her, Star. If you can't live with her as she is, you should send her away...or leave yourself!"

When I said that, her shoulders sagged, and she turned to me. "Would you send me away, Spearl?"

"You might not want to ask me that right now," I told her.

Quickly, she walked around me toward the door, trying to hide her tears. Before she left, without turning around, she said, "She can change herself, Spearl, the way I used to erase...when Earline..." Unable to finish that sentence, she walked out of the kitchen, then out of the house.

Gently, I tapped on Kimikin's door. "It's Daddy, sweetie. I have something for you, and for Claireth."

After a minute, the door opened a bit and Kimi slipped out, closing it behind her. She was wearing a little robe. "Claireth's sleeping. I don't think she's well."

"Maybe I can help," I said.

"Can you cure FireSprites?" she asked in a sad voice. "Can you make them human?"

I knelt and took her in my arms. At first she tensed, but finally embraced me back. "I *love* you, Kimikin! And I love what you love. You're my daughter, and I've always thought you were pretty as can be. If anything, you're only prettier, now."

"Oh, Daddy!" she said, hugging me close. "Don't ever go away again. Don't leave me with her. She *hates* me, and she hates Claireth!"

"She doesn't," I told her. "She's confused. She's been through a lot, more than you can know. So much that she needed a lifetime with the Fierae to get well. To be honest, I fear for her..."

When I didn't finish, Kimi said, "...Sanity. Yes, Daddy, I think you should. She's obsessed with changing me. And now, more than ever, I *mustn't* change." Then she took my hand, placed it on her belly and smiled. "There may be a grandbaby in there."

"Are you sure?" I asked "With Claireth? How is that possible?"

"I told you, we're FireSprites. We don't have to do it the messy way," she said through an adorable giggle. "And, no, I'm not sure. But there's reason to believe, and I'll know for certain soon. I fear the idea of being pregnant without a home, but I'll leave here before I'll allow Mother to come between Claireth and me. *Look* at me, wearing this robe! Mother put that in my head, and it's *obscene!*" she said, tearing the garment from her body. "Now I need to sleep. We only come out at night."

"Wait!" I told her. Then I found my pack and gave her the gifts that were in it.

"I love my muley," she said, hugging it to her. "And Claireth will love her FireSprite. Or maybe it's a *Dakini temptress!*" she said, giggling again. "It will mean a lot that you thought of her, Daddy."

XXVI
Sister

I went looking for Star, but only found her when I looked up. She was high in a Zephre cocoon. I was angry and tired and heartsick for Kimi. I summoned up talent that called for Blitz' blood, took over Star's Zephrae and drew her to me. I could see her hold out her arms, shocked that she was moving sideways as well as down. When she landed in front of me, I shooed away her chorus of Zephrae. "How?" she said, a shocked look on her face.

"Anger!" I told her, and she actually seemed frightened. Then I calmed and said, "No. I'm not angry with you, Star. I'm angry with my *sister*. I'm angry with what you used to be, because I see my poor sister, confused and feeling betrayed, coming back. And I won't allow it. I could pluck your light-body from you, Star, and send you back to the Fierae in an instant." When her eyes went wide, I said, "Yes, there's much I can do that you're not aware of. Maybe even more that *I'm* not aware of."

"Would you do it, Spearl? If you sent me back, I don't think I'd ever be able to return to you. Even now, I hear the Fierae call."

When she said that, something just broke inside me, and I grabbed her into a fierce embrace. *"Please*, Star, come to terms with our daughter. She thinks she might be..."

"What, Spearl? Pregnant? You don't believe that tripe, do you? It's Claireth stringing her along. *They* did that to her. *Claireth* did that to her. What were her reasons? Can you be sure?"

I released Star and took her by the shoulders. "I love my daughter *as she is*, Star. Claireth is now a daughter to me as well. If you can't control the bigotry of your mind, you *will* hold your tongue."

"You're threatening me, Spearl," she said, tears beginning to fall.

"I'm *warning* you, Star, for all our sakes. Accept our daughter, accept who she loves. Let go! Your fear has become anger and is threatening to become hate. If I see hatred, I'll act. That is a *serious* warning, both to you *and* to me. Because if I lose you, Star—

again—I'll grieve for the rest of my life. And I'll live out the rest of it only for Kimikin."

XXVII
Luminae

Late that night after Daddy came home, Claireth and I crept out of the house. Though she'd been happy with Daddy's gift, and also that he'd said he loved her, Claireth didn't seem well. She doesn't glow in our world, but even the glitter of her skin seemed faded and I couldn't see a bit of dust on her. "What's wrong?" I asked her as we sat on a sandy place by the pond.

She didn't seem to hear me, and I could feel her shaking a tiny bit. Looking down at the sand, she said, "Paw prints."

"All sorts of creatures come here to drink," I told her. Then I hugged her to me and asked again, "What's wrong, my poor darling, what's *wrong*?"

Suddenly, Claireth began to shake in earnest, and she whispered, "He's here."

Then I noticed those two eyes glowing, and heard his light say, "I've come for you." He had a mushroom in his mouth, which he laid on the ground. "I have a secret place set aside in the BorderRealm. Do as I tell you and go with me now, or this one's life is forfeit. Actually, she'll die of this world soon, anyway. But unless you want to see her with her throat torn out, take a tiny bite of this mushroom and come with me."

"I'll burn you to a cinder," I growled.

"You can do that," he said, "and I'd actually love to see you wield fire. But you'll only burn this little fox. Soon I'll come back in another and finish it. Maybe I'll creep into your room—I've already been there, you know—and bleed her dry while you're sleeping beside her. Don't be foolish, little lady. I won't hurt you. You will be *exalted*, and cared for, and will rule a kingdom. Wouldn't you like to be my Queen?"

I didn't care what this creature said, as my fire rose and my eyes burned bright. I was going to roast him slowly and see if he'd want to come back for more of *that*. But suddenly my fire settled completely, and Claireth beside me sighed as if in great relief. Then a light appeared over the pond, and a form walked toward us over the water.

The light of the fox said, "I *will* have you!" and then he was gone.

The form over the water became a beautiful man...or a boy. Or a girl, a woman. I couldn't be sure. It came to us, and I suddenly realized Mother and Daddy were coming over the ridge.

The beautiful being lifted Claireth into his arms—appearing now to be a man. Mother and Daddy came running up, and Daddy said, "We could *feel* it, it was *calling.*"

"How could you bring this poor child here?" he said.

"She came of her own accord, and..." Mother began.

But the man interrupted her and said, "You gave her the means and incentive. You may as well have reached into her world and snatched her out of it. She can't live here. She's dying, can't you see?"

"Please help her," I begged.

"I'll take her home and she'll be fine," he said, smiling at me. His smile was like light, palpable light that shined into me, and I felt an incredible peace. In a calm voice, I said, "I'm coming, too."

"I won't take you," he said. "I don't shuffle flesh between worlds. But that which stole you into the BorderRealm has set things in motion that have made you of that world as well."

"Who are you?" Mother asked in a hushed voice.

"Luminae," Daddy breathed.

"Some say," the man answered. "The thousand years are almost up, and the Third will try again to rule men with greed."

"Is that fox one of the Third?" Mother asked.

The man smiled and said, "*Fox?* He's a jackal, the Lord of the Third, and he wants Kimikin. He wants an aneke'lemental. Since there is only one other, you should be wary as well," he said, and I knew he was talking to Mother. "Perhaps you should both return to the Fierae, though I would not force such a thing." Then he turned and walked out over the pond with Claireth in his arms. He became brighter and brighter, until he vanished. Suddenly, we were in the dark again. I walked over and picked the mushroom off the ground. "Kimi! Wait!" Mother said.

But it was already in my mouth. As I was falling away into the BorderRealm, I said, "Don't call me Kimi, Mother!"

79

XXVIII
Home away from Home

As soon as I stepped foot in that world, I saw the light-being, the Luminae, still carrying Claireth. She was already looking much better. The Luminae was a tall, beautiful girl, now, or a beautiful boy, I didn't know until she spoke. "I knew you'd follow," she said to me. "I'm sorry I could not bring you. There's no need to consume that poison anymore. You're a marvelous creature, Kimikin FieraeGirl. We'll protect you when we can, but I haven't the license to destroy that one. In this world, or the other, you must hide. Among the HalfFire here, you'll be hard to find. If you go back, you should shed your FireSprite form and hide as a human."

"I wouldn't change if I could," I told her.

Then, suddenly, she seemed to realize something and threw her head back in laughter. It was a sound that made me feel wonderful and light and airy. Then she came to me and touched my belly. "Yes, I guess you'd better stay as you are. The Realms will commingle again, it seems. Once more, beauty arrives from foul intentions. We will come to see you when he arrives. We will bless this blessing."

"We're home!" Claireth shouted, jumping down out of the beautiful girl's arms.

"What's your name?" I asked the Luminae.

The girl glowed brighter and said, "Ariel, some say."

I knew she was about to leave us, and said, "Thank you for saving me from the fox!"

"I came only to rescue the HalfFire child." Then she smiled luminously, and said, "My timing was auspicious."

When she vanished, Claireth wrapped me in her arms and covered me with kisses. "Are you okay?" I asked her.

For answer, she placed her palm on my belly and said through a wicked grin, "I want one, too."

Claireth spun us down to tiny, rubbed her hands on her arms and sprinkled me with dust. It felt *incredible*! "Now it's back to work!" she announced, pure joy in her voice. "We're Rovers and must patrol the Realm! Keeping on the move will also outfox the fox."

"But *I'm* not a Rover," I told her.

"I'm a First among Rovers, and can appoint whom I please. Are you serious? Will you take the oath?"

"What's the oath?" I asked.

"I promise to patrol the BorderRealm until I'm no longer a Rover."

"And how do you become no longer a Rover?" I said.

"You quit!" she told me, as if I'd asked a silly question.

Solemnly, I pledged, "I promise to patrol the BorderRealm until I'm no longer a Rover."

"Oh! You're one of us now!" Then she whispered to me, "You don't, by any chance, know who we report to, do you?"

Although we were always on duty, we were also always a hairsbreadth away from tackling each other into a love tussle. Finally, the hairsbreadth broke, and we *Fluttered*. "You know, you *do*!" Claireth said as we began that lovely flight.

"Do?" I asked

She placed her hand on my belly and said, "*Do!* Have one! Here!"

"Kinda figured," I smiled.

Then she grinned to beat all helluva and said, "Now me! They'll be such wonderful playmates!"

"But what if they have human in them, or aneke'lemental, not just FireSprite?" I asked, that thought coming back around from my argument with Mother.

"Oh! They will! They'll have everything *we* have. They'll be *us, together,* but little and cute and cuddly. And they'll grow up to be First Rovers!"

"They'll grow up to be whatever they *want* to be," I told her.

"Of course," she said, "but you wouldn't deny me a fantasy, would you?"

"Maybe *I'm* your fantasy."

"Let's find out," she said, grinning again. "Fantasy girls can't spark a babe!"

With nothing to stop us this time, we let our FlutterLove take us where it would. Sparks definitely flew.

XXIX
Grappling

Star and I walked back over the ridge in silence. Finally, I said, "Luminae. What *are* they?"

"We need to speak to the Fierae again," Star said.

"Not *me*!" I told her. "Not any time soon!"

"I know," she whispered, her head down and tears falling. "Why, Spearl, do I love her so much when she leaves us, and treat her so badly when she's here? *Am* I insane? Maybe I *should* return to the Fierae."

"Do you love me?" I asked.

"More than you know."

"Then I'll grapple with you, if I must, to keep you. Because I love you, too."

"We need to go find her again, Spearl."

"We need to be *careful*!" I told her. "That Luminae spoke benignly, but I heard warning in his voice."

"It was a *she*, I think," Star said.

"Whatever. I don't think it would be happy with us if Claireth ended up here again. He...or she...seemed very protective."

"I hope she protects Kimikin," Star said. "She wouldn't take Kimi with her, did you notice? Maybe she thought our daughter should stay here."

"And maybe she'd like to see all aneke'lementals go to the Fierae. She said something about that, too."

"I'm going to find majick that will let us stay there, at least for a longer time," Star told me. "If nothing else, I have to make peace with my child. Even if I can't, I still want to protect her. I'm seriously not happy about this fox thing. The Luminae called him a Jackal."

"Then cogitate, Star. Eat and sleep and get *strong*! Keep your mind-sea calm. When we go this time, we must be prepared. We have to know our reasons and motives, because I think these Luminae are concerned with those things. I think they're a high order of being, Star."

"But isn't this fox, this jackal, a Luminae as well?"

"I don't know," I told her. "He's the Lord of the Third, whatever that means."

"We *need* to speak to the Fierae," she repeated.

"Then talk to ground charges—all day if you want, for all the good it will do. You can't come out of your body to converse with whole Fierae and neither can I. Not yet. When I can I will."

"I'm sorry, Spearl," Star said, putting her fingers to her temples. "Keep grappling with me. It's *you* who keep me sane."

Hugging her to me as we walked up onto the porch, I said, "Something to eat, something to drink, and a long sleep. I'll bet there's excellent Maria in Kimikin's room."

"Corn and Maria," Star said. "Yes, I'd like to forget for just a little while."

I tried, and so did Star, to clear her mind—to calm her sea. She exercised her majick daily, calling lines and Zephres and storms, and flocks of birds that dimmed our daylight. She threw fire into the sky that dissipated in sheets over the horizon. At night, she stood in the yard and called up the Linea Clipses, sometimes holding them so long that World seemed to shiver. Then I would call to her, "Enough!" and she'd cease immediately.

I fed her liver every day, and spinach and collards and bloody red cow. I concocted a tonic of Molasses and wine and a touch of ferrite. She was radiant and magnificent, her amethyst eyes always bright and alive. Her skin glistened, and she was warm to the touch.

One night, in bed, she threw her arm over me, gave me a kiss, and said, "Thank you, Spearl. I'm Starshine FieraeBorn again. Now we must take care of *you*."

"So I can talk to the Fierae?" I said.

"Too soon, my darling," Star told me. "Much too soon. I'll feed you and hold you while you sleep, and wait with you the proper length of time between joinings. I miss my daughter, but my passion is under control. Do you trust me?" she asked.

"I've *always* trusted you, Star. Even when I didn't."

"I know," she said, laying her head on my chest. "It's your trust that saves me."

In the morning, I found Star in the kitchen with a cup of tea. Her eyes were closed and her face relaxed. She was either meditating or cogitating. I made tea for myself, took a slug of the molasses tonic, and sat. "I have an idea," she said without moving or batting an eye.

"Let's hear it," I said.

"Can you remember—from Papa's memories—when he met Mama on a bridge she'd constructed between their mind-seas?"

"Our parents' memories aren't as clear to me now that I'm in this body, but I think I know what you mean."

"I'd show you a trace of it," Star said, "but you'd only see Mama and Papa in their bed in Ginny. Light bodies don't trace, and they were in their light bodies on that bridge. Tonight, I'll build such a bridge, and call you to meet. We can examine each other closely, maybe see a shadow of what our light bodies became when we went to the BorderRealm. If I could see that, my crossing majick would be very strong."

"Makes sense. Will you make me pancakes?"

"I've a premonition," Star said, standing up out of her chair. "Something tells me Spearl's hungry."

That night, before bed, I found Star in the kitchen brewing a little pot of something with a blue tint. I looked at her and she said, "A potion to help me build my bridge tonight."

"It's blue," I said.

"Very gently blue, yes. It's an ingredient."

"Alright," I said, trusting her. "I'm sleepy. See you in my dreams."

"You will," she said. "I'll be coming for you."

I was dreaming of Star's ring—the Universe ring she still wears. Then I saw her wearing *only* her ring on its braided gold chain. She was stepping out onto a silvery bridge over an ocean of mist. "Come to me, my love. Come wearing only your love for me."

I found myself on that bridge with her, and she said, "You know not to touch me, don't you? You know where you are?"

"Your light-body is magnificent," I told her. "I haven't seen it in fifteen years."

"You look like Thirest," she told me. "Shake it off."

I removed the residual stain of Thirest's body, and Star whimpered, "Spearl! Oh, Spearl, how I love you!"

"Careful, now," I said. "Remember where you are."

"Yes," she said, immediately recovering her control. "Let me examine you, and you look me over carefully. Look for residual of what we became."

"You're very easy to look at," I told her.

"And you," she smiled. "I hope we wake up soon."

We kept a respectable distance between us—if we touched we'd be gone, our light would mingle and *poof!* I looked and looked at Star, but saw only her bright beauty in front of me. At some point, however, she bent forward and began looking intently into my navel. From the intensity of her gaze, I knew she was seeing *something*.

Then she started to fall toward me! I leapt backward to keep us from touching, and seemed to tumble off the bridge. I was falling through endless mist, and for a moment it frightened me. That moment was all it took. I was gone, and far removed from my mind.

XXX
Dakini

Claireth and I were in a teaberry patch, munching huge, pulpy berries the size of watermelons. "They make your breath so *sweet!*" Claireth told me.

"Let me taste yours!" I said.

That was about to become a frolic, when we both heard buzzing. Something was coming. "Dakini!" Claireth said.

"How do you know?" I asked.

"I'm a Rover. Remember that sound. Those are *outcast* Dakini. Most Dakini are good, though you didn't hear that from me. But a very few are renegade. They *wear* things, and sometimes take Fairae and play with them whether they like it or not. They've never tried that with a FireSprite, but I'd just as soon have nothing to do with them."

"They *rape* Fairae?" I said. "Shouldn't we stop them?"

"If we caught them at it, we'd have to take them to be locked away. But it would probably become a fight to the death."

"They'd kill us?"

"They'd try," Claireth smiled.

Then they came down, six of them, wearing scarves, and ribbons tied round their arms and thighs and waists. Slowly, they folded their wings and circled us. "Rovers?" one of them said.

"We are," I told him. "And *not* in the mood for your shite!"

"Ooooo! You're feisty!" Claireth chirped with a smile.

"They're LoveLocked," a girl Dakini said. "They'll fight for each other fiercely."

Then she pointed at me and said, "I think *you* have a little human in you."

"Let's put a little Dakini in her," the boy said, leering and laughing.

That one who was threatening rape was standing next to an enormous teaberry. Quicker that Fierae spit, I summoned my fire and boiled the berry till it exploded. Hot, minty pulp knocked that Dakini to the ground, and the others retreated many paces. "You *smell* better now!" I yelled at the felled thug.

"'That's no FireSprite," the girl said.

"We can't take her," another called. "Let's just go tell him where she is."

"Yeah," the girl answered. "Like she's going to stay put till he gets here!"

"I'll go get him," a different girl said. "You all stay here and keep her from leaving."

When I heard that, and realized they were in league with the fox, my fire rose of its own accord. I'd never felt it so hot—I felt *molten*! "Five seconds and you die!" I said, my voice gone elemental.

"Go get him," the one I'd bathed in berry shouted. "*I'll* keep her here!"

Two other Dakini joined him. Three fled into the air. "Just stay put," the berry boy growled at us, and I noticed long, sharp, vicious claws growing from his fingers.

Then I saw that Claireth's hands were similarly daggered. "Not going to happen!" I bellowed, and three Dakini glowed white for a second, then fell to ash.

My fire was vehement, and it was all I could do to settle it. Claireth's eyes were wide watching me, as I felt my inferno calm. Finally, she said, in an awed voice, "You were *human* again, Cutie Pie! For just an instant, you were the way I found you!"

I watched as Claireth's claws withdrew, and also noticed fangs retreating to tooth-size. "You're a little tiger!" I smiled.
"And you are quicksilver ablaze! You're a wonderful, powerful witch, my Cutie Pie, and a shape changer!"

"I don't like that I killed," I told her. "But *rape*! I put that one out of his misery."

"You gave them fair warning," she said. "And *that one*! I'd have slashed him to the depth of my claws and smiled. Now we need to fly! I'm sure you know who they've gone to get."

"I'll singe his arse, too!" I said.

"You can't kill one of those, Cutie Pie," she said in a harsh whisper. "Now let's go!"

After flying a good distance (I was getting much better at it), Claireth declared that she wanted a victory feast. Telling me to make a fire (apparently, she's my superior Rover), she fluttered off. I had a fire going in a few nannyseconds, and she came back shortly dragging a dead mouse by the tail.

She was strong and fast, and produced a wicked claw, which she wielded with precision. Before long, a skinned haunch of mouse was roasting, and Claireth was crushing herb leaves and sprinkling them over it. Watching her cook, I asked, "Should we really be celebrating killing those Dakini?"

"No," she told me. "We're celebrating still being alive. And I don't know about you, but it doesn't hurt me to eat after calling up my fighting form."

"Is that majick?" I asked.

"Of a sort," she told me. "I extend my luminous to claws and fangs, and whatever other armaments I may want, then slow it to creature. After battle, it reverses. But we don't get majick-starved the way you used to, just a little hungry."

"I should be a lot hungry, after calling up that much fire," I said. "Actually, I should be craving that mouse's liver."

"The surgeons fixed that," Claireth smiled. "Whenever you walk now, you take metal from the ground."

Without warning, Claireth fluttered off again, but quickly returned carrying an enormous blueberry. "These go good with mouse," she smiled, gazing longingly at our now roasted dinner. She looked so cute as her little fangs grew out a tiny bit.

Herbed roast mouse and blueberry is fine fare. Claireth and I lounged, hands on each other's full tummies, and drowsed. At some point, I said to her, "Tell me what you know about the Luminae."

"Very little," she said, wiggling her fingers to cause me a lovely distress. "The nice Luminae pretty much stay in RealmWhite. When they appear here, it's usually to do a good deed or needed service. I'd never seen one cross into the outward light before, but then, I've never known a FireSprite to need rescuing from that place, either.

"The others, like that fox, must stay here. They've been bound here for a very long time, and their light diminished so they can only manifest small animals. But recently, their light began growing again—some faster than others. They become larger and larger animals. Though he seems to like fox, I think that one could be a wolf. Maybe even a boy or a girl."

"What did the Luminae mean, back in my world, when he said the thousand years are almost up?"

"I don't remember her speaking in your world. Something was killing me. And I hope *this* can be your world now. I just can't *live* in the outward light, Cutie Pie," she pouted. Then she smiled again, took my hand that was on her belly, and made me rub. "I'm a fat grape, here," she giggled. "But that place was making me a *raisin!*"

"Let me kiss this fat grape," I said, smooching and tonguing her tummy.

"Please don't start my fire!" she begged. "I'm so *full!*"

XXXI
Fallen Deep

I could see, as if from a distance, Star hovering over me. She was saying something, but I couldn't hear. Though I felt myself moving to speak, to rise up out of bed, my body didn't move. I was fallen deep into the sea of my mind. I needed to rise.

Star was saying something over and over, trying to make me understand, mouthing her words slowly. "Don't struggle," I believe she was saying, and then I must have slept.

Eventually, sleep lifted, though I can't say how long it lasted. Vaguely, I became aware that Star and Lizabeth were standing beside the bed. I could hear them, somewhat, as if they were far away and speaking through thick, cotton mufflers. "Just *stay* with him!" Star was saying. "...like a fever. *Talk* to him."

"Could I *catch* it, Auntie Star?"

Star took Lizabeth by the shoulders, and I thought she might shake her. For some reason, this seemed funny. But I could no longer hear them, could no longer stay awake, could no longer be sure of who I was.

The next time I became aware (or less than aware), I saw Wanda May. The look on her face was pure fear. I couldn't hear at all again, but it was obvious that Star was shouting angrily at her. Then Star put Gryn in Wanda's hand, and for a moment, I heard. "Because it doesn't like me!" Star said, angry again.

The bed shook, or I shook, or *something* shook, and then I felt the ice-cold blade of Gryn on my forehead. Slowly, I began to hear again—strange words, some like the first Starshine used to speak—and I could see Wanda May sweating, her eyes rolling up beneath fluttering eyelids. Then she collapsed, and Star caught her. "He'll come back now," I heard Wanda May say, as Star helped her stand.

"Sorry I yelled at you," Star said, hugging her.

"I wish you two would be more careful!" Wanda May scolded in an exhausted voice. "Fugging around with the Linea Clipses, wanting to change people, playing games over your mind-sea! I'm just an Apprentice, Star. Y'all mustn't expect such majick from me."

"You're a *mighty* Apprentice, Wanda May," Star told her, kissing her hard on the lips.

Then Wanda, blushing, said, "I need to get home! I've a village full of pregnant girls to tend!"

"So you're thriving," Star said, caressing Wanda's cheek affectionately.

"Thriving with *horniness!*" Wanda May chuckled. "But, yes, we do well. Thank Spearl again for curing those chicken pox."

"He ate every one of the treats the mothers gave him."

"Didn't save you a *one*?" Wanda said, squinting her eyes.

"Not a one," Star lied.

Once I was risen from my sea, I felt fine. But both Star and Wanda May insisted I stay in bed for one more sleep. "Lizabeth's in Kimikin's room, probably full of Maria. I'm taking Wanda May back. It's the least I can do."

"It'd take me two days by myself," Wanda May said. "Still, it's a little scary when you ride us over the forest like that."

"I *might* could teach you that trick someday," Star told her.

"Don't get her hopes up, Star," I said.

"She's a *very* strong Apprentice, Spearl. She just doesn't know it."

"Someday," Wanda May smiled, obviously doubting she could learn the trick as much as I did. I knew *I* had never been able to do it.

"*Stay in bed!*" Star demanded as they left. "If you want anything, call Lizabeth. I'll take *her* home as soon as I get back."

I wasn't sleepy. I wanted some wine. I was just about to disobey, and get up to find some when Lizabeth poked her head into the room. She was grinning, and had definitely been into the Maria. When she saw I was awake, she came in and said, "Hello, Uncle Spearl."

Actually, as Spearl, I'd been her grandfather. I left that body when she was three.

"Hello, Lizabeth. You seem happy."

"Kimikin grows just the bestest l'il ol' buds," she said, sitting on the bed. "Want me to get you one?"

"How about getting me a mug of wine?" I said.

"You know," Lizabeth told me, lightly touching her fingers to the blanket over my thigh, "in that body, you and I aren't related at *all*."

Lizabeth was pretty, and I wanted her to stay that way. "Do you know," I told her, "that your Auntie Star has a jealous streak."

"Jealousy is a *terrible* thing," she said.

"I *know*!" I agreed. "But it just seems to run in her family. Did you ever hear about how the first Starshine once strangled a woman just for looking at her lover Spaul?"

"*Strangled?*" Lizabeth yelped, removing her hand.

"I'm afraid even strangling might not sate your Auntie's jealousy."

"I'll get you some wine, Uncle Spearl," she said.

"That's a good girl."

I really shouldn't assign to Star the moniker of Jealous Woman. She knows the difference between play and Binding Love. I know of at least two occasions since we've been together as life-mates when Star played with another—both times it was a woman, both times Wanda May. I haven't, but I am, after all, on my second life and... okay, I still miss Kimmy. And I *have* Star. Though I did wonder why Star hadn't, at least once, brought Wanda May into our bed.

Had I allowed Lizabeth's advances, it would only have mattered because it was Lizabeth. Star had actually always loved the girl dearly, but felt betrayed when she and Kimikin became lovers. Had it happened, Star would never have said a word to me about it, but afterward I'd have felt some trepidation about leaving the two of them alone together. When you're as powerful as Star, sometimes you just don't know your own strength.

"Here's your wine, Uncle Spearl," Lizabeth said, handing me the mug and scooting back out of the room. She really is a pretty girl.

With Wanda May flown back to her village, and Lizabeth back at the Crossing, things returned to normal. Yes, that was a joke. I hadn't known normal in years, and recently, normal had become a punchline. Here's the joke: There's another world, full of lovely winged Sprites and Luminae. My daughter was stolen *into* that world, and is now a possibly pregnant FireSprite named Jilhannah of the Clan

Fiereste. What's more, the father is perhaps an even *cuter* girl-child FireSprite named Claireth. Punch-line: *Normal!*

But Star had a plan (she always did), and told me what she'd seen before she knocked me off the bridge into Shangri-la-la-land. "I saw how your light-body changed!" she told me. "It turned inside out from the navel!"

"What?" I asked, trying *not* to picture that.

"It draws in at the navel, like a drain. Your light goes down it, then comes out the other side."

"And it's inside out?"

"I don't know how else to put it Spearl. Our light bodies glow, *are light,* but here, we ourselves are not the source of that light. When we're *there,* we *are* the source. Light comes *to* us here, and comes *from* us there."

"So, it's confusing," I smiled.

"I can do it, Spearl. When we cross, a tiny conduit between our light bodies there and the residual that stays here remains open. The light that we *give* from there, flows to what *takes* here and eventually ends up sucking us back across. I can plug that conduit!"

"So it's *very* confusing," I said.

"Do you really not see it?" she asked.

"I see it," I told her. "How long will we be able to stay?"

"As long as nothing taxes me, and I can keep the conduit plugged indefinitely. It will take some effort, so I may not be able to work much other majick at the same time. But I can keep us there, Spearl! We can find her!"

"When do you want to try this?"

"One more sleep. In the morning." Then she kissed my forehead and I felt her touch my thought for just a second, thinking I wouldn't notice.

"Stop that!" I told her.

"I didn't..." she began. Then her eyes squinted and she said, "That little brat made a pass at you, didn't she?"

"Did you stay very long at Wanda May's when you took her back?" I asked pointedly.

"I did *not!*" she insisted. "And even though I *wouldn't* be jealous, I'm glad you didn't either."

XXXII
Rover Byron

Claireth and I were fluttering high up in the starry night sky. I think we both had FlutterLove on our minds, but when we got up there it was just so beautiful that we hovered and stared. To the west, the hills were glowing darkly against the starlit sky. "There's the moon," Claireth said, pointing.

"I don't see it," I told her.

"It's the place with no stars...that circle, see?"

"Do you see those hills?" I said. "That's where I was going when all this began."

"A long way off, though not if we fly fast."

"I wanted to see all of it along the way," I told her.

Claireth smiled. "We can go there. And it's good for you to walk a bit."

"And love a bit?" I smiled back.

Then we Fluttered beneath that lightless moon.

Sometimes we walked, sometimes we flew, always heading west. One drawn, we saw another Rover in the distance, a boy Sprite named Byron. "Ahoy Rover Claireth!" he called.

"Ahoy Rover Byron," she laughed. "Byron's a gas," she said to me. "Pure ether! You'll like him."

When he caught up to us, Claireth told him, "This is Jilhannah, a new Rover."

Conspiratorially, Byron said to us both, "I know who she is, Claireth. I'm a Rover, after all."

"How many Sprites know?" I asked, concerned.

"Does it really matter?" he said. "We know you two are strongly LoveLinked. We'd never do anything to hurt Claireth. Or you," he added.

"We're more than LoveLinked," Claireth told him, grinning at me.

"*LoveLocked!*" Byron said, looking her over. "Yes, I see it now!"

"That's not all," Claireth told him.

"What?" he asked.

After a little anticipation-stoking silence, Claireth cried out, "We're sparked!" Her smile was so huge I thought the top of her head would slide off.

"Both?" Byron exclaimed. "A wonderment! Claireth HalfFire, bravest Rover ever, has become even braver! You're BornHome bound!"

"What's BornHome?" I asked.

"Where you two will be soon enough," Byron smiled. Then he became serious, and said, "I'm proud to love you, Claireth, First Rover. And I'm proud to love Fourth Rover Jilhannah!"

"Call me Jil," I blushed.

"Proud to love you, Byron!" Claireth grinned "Now tell us about *you*! Still LoveLinked to half the girls in ClanHome?"

"Can you keep a secret?" he asked.

"Secrets don't seem to hold water around here," I said.

"You're no secret, Jilhannah. Everyone knows you're here, but only a few know what you look like. I'm the only one that knows your new name, and not fang or claw would get it out of me. You two should know, I've heard rumor that outcast Dakini are trying to find you."

"They found us," Claireth told him. "Three of them died."

"Fang and claw?" Byron asked in an awed tone.

"Fierae girl fire," she said. "Didn't have to dip a fang."

"They attacked you?"

"Claws out, and they threatened to play with us like it or not. The messy way!"

"And I know you don't care for it," he said.

"Even the other way," Claireth told him, "I'd not want to be *forced!*"

"A *terrible* thing!" Byron agreed. "I'm sorry they had to die, but I'm glad they're dead."

"Me too," Claireth said.

"Me three," I chimed in, and you'd think I'd just told the funniest joke in World, the way those two laughed.

"So what's the secret?" Claireth asked Byron as the three of us walked.

Almost whispering, he said, "I've a very strong LoveLink with a Faerae girl."

"No!" Claireth said. "Is she lovely?"

"Sweeter than bee pollen," he said.

"I'm so happy for you," Claireth told him. "The clans are mixing again, and it's good. I know we joke about each other, but we're all HalfFire, after all."

"It's true," Byron said. "The old Glamour War rivalries are fallen away. Half the babes in BornHome are mixed, and they take in any Dakini or Fairae mothers who show up."

"Really? I didn't know that. I patrol constantly and just haven't kept up with things," Claireth told him. "But I'm glad. They say it's a long, hard pain in the end. We should help any who ask."

"I hadn't considered the long, hard pain," I said to Claireth.

"But after, you get a babe!" she smiled. "And your pain will turn to wildflower perfume and cricket song!"

Byron told us he was heading west, and would travel with us a while. "I've been patrolling to the east," he said. "Now I'm heading to ClanFair."

"Is that where she is?" Claireth giggled.

"Yes," Byron said, his eyes gone distant. "Her name is Titanya. She has moon dark eyes that draw me in."

"Ooooooh," Claireth cooed. "Byron and Titanya! Maybe you'll start a new clan! Clan FairSprite!"

"I'd like to go see some Fairae," I said. "The only ones I've met are the two who taunted us."

"Prissi and Teali, no doubt," Byron said.

"I *think* that's their names," Claireth told him.

"Most Fairae are *not* like those two," he said. "And, hey, I know some Sprites who are real mouse arses, too."

Claireth and Byron laughed at that. Then Claireth said through her laughter, "Eldrich!" and both of them squealed.

When their laughter settled, Byron said, "Yes, come with me to ClanFair, you two! Three brave Rovers in the village at once— they'll toast us with mead!"

"And give us some?" Claireth asked.

"Of *course* they'll give us some!"

XXXIII
ClanFair

The HalfFire of ClanFair greeted us warmly. Though there are no Fairae Rovers, they appreciate those who patrol the realm, and even have a little corps called Raptors who keep watch over ClanFair. Some of those Raptors gave us mead, and told tales of frightening off outcast Dakini. After a while, we were pretty drunk, and I said, "I wish I had some Corn to give y'all!"

When they looked at me funny, I said, "It's a drink much more powerful than mead."

"Ah," one of the Raptors said. "I'll bet it's not strong as elderberry distillate."

"It's so strong," I told him, "that if you drop a jug of it, it might 'splode!" I was slurring my words and giggling about it.

"Well, I *have* some elderberry," the Raptor told me, producing a small jar. "Take a sip!"

He handed me the jar and I took a slug. "Respectable," I said, trying to catch my breath, and everyone laughed harder.

Before long, our rowdy troupe wandered away from the village and built a bonfire. Then I noticed a group of four or five Raptors playing at love. "Where'd Byron go," I asked Claireth.

"Off with Titanya," she said with a hiccup. Then we noticed one of the Raptors looking over at us. "Come play!" he called,

"Come on, Cutie Pie," Claireth said, standing drunkenly. "Let's go show them how Rovers love!"

"Should we?" I asked, giggling again.

"If you think of a reason why not," she said, "tell me tomorrow!" Then she threw an arm around me and led me off to what looked very much like an orgy.

I was a real helluva raisin' Rover that night—cocky and sure. When I came to, I was hung over and sore. Claireth woke at the same time. She had one arm around me, and her other around a snoring Fairae boy. Liberating her arm from under the Raptor, she helped me up and said, "Let's go, I'm played out."

"My *head*! Gol*lam*!" I swore.

Claireth sprinkled her dust on me, which helped immensely, and said, "Let's head for the hills. After the time we gave them, they're sure to wake up wanting more."

I couldn't remember the time we gave them at all, and wasn't sure I wanted to know.

We started out walking, as Claireth said it would do us good. "Specially you. Some fresh metal in your blood won't hurt."

When I was silent for a long time, Claireth asked, "What's wrong, Cutie Pie?"

"I can't really remember what we did last night," I told her. "And I'm wondering if we should have done what I can't remember."

"Hmmmm," Claireth pondered. Finally she said, "Some are bashful after playing at LovePile. If *you* are, you shouldn't drink so much mead, and no elderberry at *all.*"

"Did we do...you know...was any of it...*messy?*"

Claireth giggled and said, "It was all pretty messy, Cutie Pie. Now stop fretting. No more LovePile for us! And it's *never* so fine as *our* love. It was just a drunken frolic, and one I'll keep you away from henceforth!" Then she giggled again.

"I wouldn't keep *you* from playing...LovePile," I told her. "I'm not *jealous*, you know."

"I'd never accuse you of such a thing," Claireth told me. "But I'd much rather have you than any dozen LovePiles, anyway. If you get drunk, though, and fall into one, I won't stop you!"

"You won't see me that drunk again," I told her.

"Then I'm glad I saw you once," she said. "You were so *funny* and so *cute!*"

"Ugh!" I moaned, and Claireth laughed to beat all helluva.

XXXIV
Hide and Seek

Sucking on each other's blue finger, we watched as the stars melted toward where dawn should be. Instead of the Ball rising, what we saw was a dark disc eating blue light.

"What do you think we should do now?" I asked Star.

"I don't know what to think, Spearl. Look up there...I feel like I'm looking at the sun's backside."

"Who knows," I said, staring at the strange Ball. "Maybe we are." Then I heard a buzzing or fluttering, and a big glowing bug flew by. I thought I heard it shout, "What in the helluva are *you*?"

"What did it say?" Star asked. When I didn't answer she yelled, "What did you say? We can't hear you!"

Suddenly, the glowing bug spun till it became a three-foot-tall, winged boy. "Oh!" Star yelped. "That's startling!"

"*I'm* startling?" The boy told her. "Look at the two of *you*! I'm going to have to report!"

"We're looking for our daughter," Star said. "Her name is..."

"Jilhanna!" I interrupted. "Of the Clan Fiereste."

"I know a few Jilhannah's," he told us. "What's she look like? And if she's a FireSprite, I don't think you two are her...hey, you're *human*, aren't you?"

"Sort of," Star told him. "And so is our daughter."

The FireSprite boy seemed to be cogitating. Finally he said with his eyes squinted, "Maybe I shouldn't be talking to you about this. How did you cross? You aren't supposed to, you know. Now go back before I report!"

Star decided to turn on some crocodile tears. She really isn't good at it, but she can produce the moisture. I was surprised when the FireSprite started dripping tears at the same moment Star did. They sparked when they hit the ground. "Stop that! Or at least wait till I leave," he pouted.

"I miss my daughter. Her name is Kimikin," Star blurted out before I could stop her.

When it was obvious that the Sprite recognized the name, Star ceased her tears, and the boy's stopped as well. "Where is she?" Star asked firmly, the feigned emotion gone from her voice.

"Find a First Rover called Claireth," he whispered. "But you should *not* say her name like that. If *he* knows you're looking for her, he'll hear and follow you." Then he leaned in close and whispered, "Rumor says Claireth and her lover fell into a LovePile in ClanFair two nights ago."

"Were they hurt?" Star asked, worry in her voice.

"In a LovePile?" he laughed. "Don't be silly. They left there the following drawn."

"What's your name?" Star asked.

"Why do you want to know?" the boy said, eyes squinted again.

"We want to know who helped us," Star told him. "And we have no friends here. It would be a comfort to know we have at least one."

What sounded like a load of shite to me, seemed to make perfect sense to the FireSprite boy. "I'm Roth, Rover Second. Claireth is my First, so if you're true, tell her I helped. If you're false—and I'll find out if you are—there'll be naught left but scraps once I've raked my claws through and torn you with fang. Now *your* names, if you're not afraid."

"I'm Star and this is Spearl," Star told him. Then she leaned in, too quickly for the little Rover to react, and kissed his forehead. I could tell there was a touch of Naiadae majick on her lips, and saw the boy smile in spite of himself. Then he backed away and started spinning till he was a bug again.

Star and I heard his tiny voice say, "Rovers will be watching you. Count on it!" Then he was gone, quick as a Fierae bolt.

XXXV
Flowers and Rumors
on the Ether

We were fluttering over a field of wildflowers in a valley near the hills. The glowing buds and petals were so beautiful they took my breath away. "Shall we drop down into them and let the perfume take us?" Claireth asked.

"Okay," I said.

Once on the ground, the smell of those flowers seemed to glow as well. It was a little bit intoxicating, like mild Maria. "It's lovely," I said, lying down under a stand of black-eyed Susans. Feeling quite relaxed, I petted Claireth's shoulders till my hands were full of dust. Then I began fondling her ears, but she didn't seem to notice. She was lost in some reverie. "What is it, sweetie?" I asked her.

"Hmmmm," she said, finally noticing my touch. "Something has crossed. Not sure where, pretty far away."

"How do you know?"

"I'm a First Rover," she smiled. "We can read the ethers a bit. If you stay a Rover long enough to become First, you'll learn."

"Could it be Mother and Daddy?"

"Lots of could be's, Cutie Pie. With all this unauthorized crossing going on, who knows. It *could* be flocks of sheep and herds of rabbit!"

"I wish I knew," I said.

"If anything comes across *near* us, I'll be on it like a flash. I'm so glad I was near when *you* came!"

"Me, too," I told her, kissing the ear I was fondling.

"Don't worry," she said. "News between Rovers travels fast. We'll come across somebody who knows more, I'm sure. Now come here and let me play with *your* ears. They're just so *cute!*"

Before we left the wildflowers, Claireth showed me certain ones we could eat. Some were sweet, others bitter, and the edible stamens out of one flower, which Claireth said were a delicacy, made me sneeze.

We drank nectar out of flowers that looked like little pitchers, which was sweet and cool. By the time we left there, I felt really refreshed. But I was also a little concerned that I wasn't more worried about Mother and Daddy. And I really thought I should be missing them (especially Daddy) at least a *bit*. But I just wasn't... couldn't. That other world was becoming a distant, unpleasant, disturbing memory. Being *human* (or some semblance thereof) seemed an alien concept as well. The more I lived as a FireSprite, the more I *felt* like a FireSprite.

Grabbing Claireth into a hug, I said through a pout, "Play with me!" Like the Fierae, I think FireSprites live to love.

After you-know-what, we decided to walk for a while, as we'd been fluttering all day (actually, all *summon*) before we found the flower-field. Claireth often worried about my "metals", and wanted my feet on the ground for a while. "I'm *fine*, Claireth," I told her. "It's not like I've been doing hard majick."

But she came up behind me, reached around and put both hands on my belly. Then she said softly, her lips on my ear, "My other babe is in here. And besides, I'm your superior Rover. You have to do what I tell you."

I leaned my head back and said, "Then why don't you tell me to..." The rest I whispered in her ear.

"Later," she told me. Then she said quietly, "Now you just keep walking, and keep talking to me as if I'm still with you. I'm going to circle around and see who's following us."

When she said that I could feel where the fear should be, but it wasn't. "Weird," I said to myself. Then, out loud for our follower to hear, I said, "So, Claireth, when do you think we'll get back to ClanFair for some LovePiling? And *elderberry*! We'll drink elderberry distillate and teach those Raptors how it's done!"

Then I heard Claireth somewhere behind say, "Gotcha!"

XXXVI
A Little Love

When the FireSprite boy vanished, I looked at Star and said, "Now what?"

"We find ClanFair," she told me.

"If we just start walking, we'll be as likely heading *away* from it as toward it," I told her.

"Why didn't you ask for directions?" she said.

"Because he was gone quicker than Fierae spit!" I answered.

"Don't be crude," she scolded.

"What was that tiny majick you smooched on his forehead?" I asked.

"Just a good feeling, Spearl. A little love."

"Well, it didn't get you any directions, did it?"

As soon as I said that, I heard a buzz zoom over us. Then a big leaf fluttered to the ground, though there were no trees overhead. I picked it up and saw something had been drawn on it in glowing liquid. There was a circle with little arrows all around it pointing in. There was also a big arrow pointing away from the circle. "What do you make of this?" I asked Star.

"It's our directions," she said with a smile. "A little love, Spearl."

Star reasoned that the circle represented that dark disc in the sky. "We face the circle east toward where that disc is rising, and the arrow points the way to ClanFair."

"Northwest," I said, after following her instructions. "Why don't we call up a Zephrae cocoon, go up and take a look around?"

"Go ahead," she said. When I just stood there, she said impatiently, "Call up a cocoon."

"*You* can't, can you?" I asked.

She remained silent, and I said, "That little Naiadae kiss was about all you could muster, wasn't it?"

A little frustrated, Star said, "*You* try clogging a conduit between two worlds! And I can do a little more than that kiss!"

"But not much," I stated, trying to impress her with that fact. I wanted her to understand our situation, *and* to be *careful*, which is like wanting Naiadae to inhabit sand.

"Are you finished?" she asked. "Will you call to the Zephrae, please."

Her slightly perturbed, slightly pouty face for some reason sparked my love, and I pecked her a kiss. "What was that for?" she asked.

"A little love, Star," I smiled.

We couldn't really see much from our cocoon. "I think they may stay tiny most of the time," I told Star. "It would make sense. You could feed three people with a blackberry."

"It looks familiar, though, Spearl—like our world at night. Look," she said, "where the Ninety-five should be. Even here, it's pretty clear of trees."

She was right, although the flora down there was glowing brighter than ours does under the fullest of moons. "Maybe we should go that way," I told her. "Go north some, then west. I won't be able to ride us over heavy forest. I might could have Gryn pull us through heavy woods, but it would be hard for you to hold onto me. Gryn pulls fast."

"Let's *not*!" Star said, and I suddenly recalled her saying to Wanda May, "It doesn't like me!"

"I prefer your other idea," she told me. "Ride us when you can, we'll hike when we must."

"Is plugging the conduit draining you now?" I asked her. "Because I put some food in my pack."

Before we'd crossed, I'd asked Star why *she* wasn't taking along a pack. "Hoping to find her quickly," she'd said. "Don't want to jinx it."

"Superstitious!" I'd smiled. "You *have* been spending time with Wanda May."

"Yes, it's draining me," Star said as I smiled at that memory. "What did you bring?"

I'd put leftover liver wrapped in a Naiadae chill, biscuits, and a skin of good wine. But when I looked in my pack, the food was not there, and the wineskin was empty. "Uh oh," I said.

"You forgot to pack it," Star said.

"Oh, I packed it," I told her. "I'm guessing food doesn't cross." I'd also packed a jar of the molasses tonic, but when I opened the lid I found just a tiny bit of sludgy liquid on the bottom. I stuck my finger in it and touched it to my tongue. "Ferrite," I said. "The rest of my tonic must have stayed behind."

"It might be for the best," Star told me. "We're *changed*, Spearl. I think if we ate food from our world, it might make us sick."

"How badly are you being drained?" I asked her.

"I'm pretty strong," she said, which didn't answer my question.

"Star!" I said, a bit angrily. "Look around! We're in a different world, and have no idea of its dangers. When I ask you a question, I need you to tell me what I need to know. The *truth*. No omissions! Do you understand me?"

I was a little harsh, but not enough to make her look like she was going to cry, which she did. "I'm sorry, Spearl," she said softly. "It's bad. In a few hours I'm going to be a mess."

Hugging her to me and stroking her beautiful curls, I said, "You're a mess all the time. I'm sorry I scolded. Just remember I love you, and *trust* me."

"I do," she said in a pitiful voice. "I just miss Kimikin *awfully*. I'll tell you everything from now on."

"Call her Jilhannah," I reminded. "Maybe I should get you to tell me everything about Wanda May," I smiled.

"You'd better stop bringing her up, or I'm going to think you're feeling guilty about Lizabeth."

"We *didn't!*" I insisted.

"I know," she smiled. "But you could still feel guilty."

I decided to take charge of our expedition, and Star didn't argue when I said, "We'll go up the Ninety-five, but before we go west, we'll go east to the sea and call out some fish. I can fill my pack with Naiadae chilled livers."

"Ugh!" Star groaned. "Since you stuffed me with them, I think I'm getting an aversion."

"Well, if you don't want to get stuffed again, you'll eat." Something about that sentence attracted me, and I said, "I wonder if loving is different here. Maybe while we're at the beach…"

"Jilhannah!" Star told me. *"After* we find our daughter!"
So much for being in charge.

As we rode the lines north, I found myself trying to picture Kimikin the way she used to be, to see her *human*. But I kept seeing her so small, and with those wings—her dark hair a tangle of ringlets, and short enough to see those interesting ears. Though her skin was glittery, it was still pale as mine...pale as Thirest's. Her eyes hadn't changed, and were so much like Star's—perhaps just a half-shade paler. She was beautiful in her winged incarnation, but it bothered me that I couldn't conjure a human image of her in my head. Then I realized it didn't matter. She was still my little girl! She was just a little littler.

XXXVII
Girl Talk

When I heard Claireth cry, "Gotcha," I spun around and into a crouch. I was about to run toward her voice, when I noticed lines of light coming from my fingertips. In a moment they solidified into little claws not half as big as the ones Claireth had sprouted. For some reason, I giggled, and my claws lit up again and disappeared back into my fingers. I wondered if I'd sprouted fangs, but when I checked with my tongue, my teeth felt normal. Then I saw Claireth coming. She had two Fairae in front of her. One of them was the girl I'd knocked down for taunting my little darling.

Claireth had a hand on each of their backs under their wings. "Come here, Rover Fourth Jilhannah," she called, "and learn a lesson. See how I'm holding these two?" When I got to her I saw that she was pinching a handful of flesh under their wings. "They can't fly while I hold them like this, or even run. The nerves in these muscles I'm holding go all the way down the backs of their legs. It's all they can do to walk where I lead them."

"And it's *hurting*!" the one called Prissi pouted.

"Why are you following us?" I said, my eyes squinted at her. "Would you like to get knocked down again?"

"You better answer her," Claireth giggled. "She's feisty for a Fourth!"

"We just saw you walking and wanted to say we were sorry. We shouldn't have teased you so."

"Why didn't you just drop down and say it then?" Claireth asked.

"Yeah!" I said. "I've heard from the ethers that you two are troublemakers!"

"Okay, Rover Jilhannah," Claireth smiled. "Calm down." Then, to the Fairae she said, "But when I let you two go, you'd better be good or I'll turn her loose on you."

When she said that, both girls became white as Fierae bolts and started shaking. "Oh, relax," Claireth told them. "She won't hurt you."

"We heard she fought three Dakini outcasts to *death! Fang and claw!*"

"That's classified Rover business!" Claireth said officiously.

"We never heard it," Prissi said.

When Claireth let them loose, Teali said, "I have some mead in this sack. Want some?"

"No!" I told her. "No mead and no LovePiles!" For some reason, I just didn't trust those two.

"What are you doing way out here?" Claireth asked, her tone gone more friendly.

"We come here sometimes," Prissy said. "We munch wild flowers in the same field you visited."

"Were you following us back then, too?" I said, and for just a second, I felt...toothy.

"No!" Teali chirped. "But we saw you'd been there."

"How'd you know it was us then?" I wanted to know. Then I ran my tongue over what were obviously becoming fangs.

Claireth noticed and put her arm around me. Then she said, softly, "It's okay, Cutie Pie. Calm down."

"I...I...we just *figured* it must have been you," Teali said, obviously a little spooked by my demeanor.

"Well, I hope you've learned a lesson," Claireth said. "Don't ever sneak up on a Rover. It's a good way to get torn. Buzz down so we can hear you coming, or give a holler."

"We will," Prissy said. "And we're really sorry we teased you. We can see you're very LoveLocked, and cute as cuddlebugs together. Can't we sit and talk a bit. We want to be friends."

"Okay," Claireth said. "And if it's still offered, I'll have a tiny taste of your mead."

There was a stand of small mushrooms nearby, and we each took a seat on one. I learned quickly that mushrooms make comfy stools, and you can reach down between your legs and pull off pieces to munch. Prissi and Teali talked about silly, Fairae girl stuff, which reminded me of Lizabeth. But after a few minutes, they gave each other a look, and Teali said, "I saw some strawberries just a quick buzz back. I'll go get us one." Then she jumped up off her mushroom and flew away.

Something wasn't right. I could feel my claws coming out. Claireth saw them, too, and said, "What's wrong, Cutie Pie?"

"Where'd she go?" I asked Prissi.

"To get a strawberry, you goose. Why don't you have some mead?"

Something was *very* wrong. I didn't need my tongue to tell that I had full-on fangs, and my claws were at least as long as I'd seen Claireth's. I jumped down off my mushroom and found myself crouched and tensed. Immediately, Claireth was beside me, clawed and fanged and casting about nervously. "What?" she said in a harsh whisper. Then we both saw the fox.

"See ya!" Prissy laughed as she flew away.

"Let's go!" Claireth cried, buzzing her wings furiously. But when we tried to fly, we found our feet held by the Terrae.

"See?" the fox said. "Already I'm learning from my little aneke'lemental."

I tried, but couldn't get the Terrae to let us go. Then I could feel them starting to make me move. "Once in my demesne," the fox purred, "I'll release your feet. There'll be no escaping once you're in your new home."

Claireth felt me starting to move and wrapped her arms around me. "Hang on tight, sweetie," I told her.

The Luminae said I didn't need blue poison anymore. I hoped she was right. Reaching deep into my majick, I worked the change that I needed in order to travel to that other world. And I brought Claireth with me. "Ahhhh!" she screamed. "It burns!"

The sun was just setting, but we were still tiny, and it seemed to hurt Claireth more than when she'd been spun up. Quickly, I tackled her to the ground and rolled her up in a sassafras leaf. "Try to relax," I said, picking her up like a sack and hugging her to me. "We've got to get out of here! He'll follow us across sure as shite!"

Working my wings like a born FireSprite, I lifted us both off the ground and flew toward the nearby hills. "I'll find shelter, Claireth, don't worry. And I'll get you back home soon, I promise!"

"This leaf smells nice," I heard her muffled voice say.

"Are you okay in there?" I asked.

"The outward light scalded my bottom," she pouted. "It'll be red as a teaberry!"

"I'll find aloe and rub it," I told her.

"Oooooooh," she cooed. "That's worth a burned bum."

XXXVIII
Escort

The fish I pulled from the sea of that world looked just like markaral, but they *glowed*! Even their livers, chilled in my pack, gave off that little shimmer of light. "They *taste* just like our markaral," Star said, making a face.

"But you feel better, don't you?" I said.

"I don't know if you could call nauseated *better*, but I'm not as weak."

"I'll cook the next one," I told her. "We'll alternate—one cooked, one raw—so it won't be so monotonous."

"But how could markaral liver ever get monotonous?" Star said sarcastically.

"Ready to head west?" I asked.

"Yes."

"No love first?" I smiled.

"If you want to have your way with me for three minutes," she said, "have at it. Otherwise, let's go find our daughter."

"Three minutes, huh?" I said. "Doesn't leave much time for foreplay."

"Time's up," Star said. "Let's go!"

In pretty short order, we flew my lines as far west as I could manage before the thickening forest stifled my majick. When I dropped the lines, and our feet, to the ground, Star started marching without missing a beat, and said, "We hike!" After a moment, she added, "If this was our world, I'd say we were heading in the general direction of Tara."

"Ilsa," I corrected.

"Let's hope so," she said. "I'd hate to find the Tara Mama and Papa found."

I'd say we hiked all night, but since it was *always* night, that might not be accurate. But just as we started talking about stopping for a short sleep, two glowing bugs buzzed us, then spun till they were human-child size. I recognized one as Roth. "You can't go any farther like this," he told us.

"Like what?" I asked.

"Gigantic!" the other Sprite said, as if I was a moron for not knowing what Roth meant.

"There are small villages through here, and not far is ClanFair," Roth told me. "You'll cause catastrophe."

"Oh! Because you're so tiny," I said.

"Duh!" the other Sprite groaned.

"This is Rover Third Willem," Roth told us, "and we'll spin you down if you give us permission."

"And if we don't give permission?" Star asked.

"Then we can't spin you, and we won't let you pass," Roth said.

"You may think you're huge," Rover Willem said, "but we're helluva fast and wickedly clawed!"

"Calm down, Rover Third," Roth soothed. "They don't look like they want to try us." Then to Star, he smiled and said, "Give permission, Lady, and I'll take you to ClanFair."

Star knelt by Roth, took his cherubic face in her hands, and kissed him. "You have our permission," she said.

I thought spinning was fun, but Star lost some of the liver she'd eaten.

XXXIX
Hiding Hole

I had Claireth clutched tight to me, and had been mostly looking straight ahead at the hills. But when I finally looked down into the deepening dusk, I saw that we were passing over a village, and tiny lights of some sort were sparking to life. "Ilsa?" I wondered out loud.

"Who's Ilsa?" Claireth mumbled from inside her leaf.

"It's a place," I told her. "We're almost to the hills. I'll find us a cave. Tiny as we are, that shouldn't be a problem."

"Don't put us down a weasel's hole," she said. "We're bite-size and can't spin up."

"I'd make weasel mince meat before I'd let him get you," I told her.

"I think you could," she said.

I found an enormous (at least to us) cave, and in we flew. Then I set Claireth down far enough inside that the last remaining rays of day couldn't touch her. I unrolled her, and got her to her feet. "Oh my!" I told her. "Your hiney *is* scorched. Lie on your tummy on your leaf. I'll be right back."

In a flash, I returned with my hands cupped full of gooey, cool aloe pulp. I was slathering it on Claireth's bottom and listening to her coo, when I saw a light farther into the cave. "Don't stop!" she said when I froze.

"Lift up your head and look," I told her.

She did, and said, "Uh oh!"

"You stay here on your tummy till I find out what it is."

"I should go with you," she said, starting to rise. But I patted her sunburned bum and she dropped back onto her belly. "Ouch!" she said. "Hey, I'm First Rover! You shouldn't be making me do things!"

"I'm First Rover till that hiney heals," I told her.

"Not fair," she said with a pout, lying her head down on the leaf.

Being tiny makes it very easy to fly, even in the outward world. I'd gotten good at doing it silently. Without a sound, I flew into the cave watching the light grow. Then I could see what looked like the inside of someone's little house. There was a fur-covered bed, a washbasin, a table, a chair, and several lit oil lamps. Against one wall of the cave leaned a bow and quiver of arrows. Over a small fire, a kettle hung. In the chair, by the fire, sat an ancient woman with skin darker brown than Mother's. Wrapping her hand with a cloth, she tipped the kettle and poured water into the small teacup she held in her other hand.

I was hovering, not making a sound, when she said, "Might as well come in. I can feel you. Can't live 'round that kinda majick all those years and not learn somethin'."

Curious now, and not frightened by this woman at all, I flew to within a few feet of her face. As soon as she saw me, she burst out laughing and said, "That's it! I'm finally, totally daft! Least I'm seein' *cute* hallucinations."

When her laughter subsided, I said, "I'm real. Honest."

"Sure," she told me. "That's just what a hallucination would say."

"If there were two of us would you believe me?" I asked.

"One hallucination, two hallucination—what's the difference? Might's well hallucinate up a whole passel of you."

Suddenly, the old woman got out of her chair and walked over to a basket that was on her table. From inside, she retrieved a round plate of glass. "Jus' the thing," she said. "Let me see you through this lens. You're cute as buttons and nekkid as Eve, aren't you?"

The old woman held her glass in front of me, and leaned in for a peek. Then she sat back in her chair and started to weep. "Star's eyes," she sobbed. "My poor, poor baby."

Claireth was still on her tummy, faithfully following doctor's orders. "C'mon," I told her. "I think I've found a good place to hide for a bit. There's a nice old lady back there."

"An old lady? In a cave?"

"Yes," I told her. "How's your bottom?"

"Fine! That aloe really worked. But maybe you should do it again, later."

114

"I'll rub it over every inch of you," I told her.

"Do I have a lot of 'inches'?" she asked.

"You're covered with them."

"Ooooooh!"

The ancient woman was still in her chair, and seemed lost in thought. Holding hands, Claireth and I hovered in front of her. "I'm back," I said, bringing her out of her reverie. "This is Claireth. I'm Jilhannah."

The lady took her glass out and held it up to us. "Y'all cutie pies for true!" she smiled.

"Yes!" Claireth told her. "We are!"

"You said I have Star's eyes," I said. "Did you know my mother?"

"I don't think even Star could make a baby like you," the old woman chuckled.

"I used to be human," I told her.

"I'm sure," she said. "I used to be a jackalope." Then she laughed again.

"What's your name?" I asked her.

"Ain't heard it spoke in so long, can't barely remember," she said.

"Is it Ilsa?" I asked.

"You should know," she smiled, "bein' my hallucination and all."

Though we couldn't convince Ilsa we were real, she seemed very pleased to have some company. "Hallucination better than nobody," she said as she scattered raisins on the table for us.

Munching one, Claireth told her, "This is what this world turns me into—a raisin!"

"Don't feel bad," Ilsa said. "It did it to me, too."

XL
Uninvited Wings

"I'm going to give you fair warning," Roth told us. "If you wear those clothes anywhere near a village, and people see you, you won't be welcome. In fact, some might chase you away."

"Our daughter told me," I said, smiling at Star. "It's considered very obscene."

"When in Rome," she said, coming out of her clothes and putting them into my pack. I did the same, but when I put my pack on, Roth said, "Don't wear that, either. Carry it."

Even respectably undressed, we received a lot of curious, though not hostile, looks. "This is the last outlier of ClanHome," Roth told us. "The villages after this are all Fairae, including ClanFair. There are FireSprite surgeons here. If you can convince them that you really are our Jilhanna's parents, they'd probably give you wings. I could order them to give them to you, but I won't."

"You're not convinced, are you?" Star asked.

"I don't know," he told her. "I think I am, but sometimes when you're not sure, doing nothing is doing best. Remember, you two are aliens searching for one of us. I'll err on the side of caution."

"You are wise," Star said, kneeling down to kiss his forehead.

"I have no intention of getting wings!" I told Star. "I don't even like being tiny and naked!"

Suppressing a smile, she said, "I just want to *talk* to these surgeons, Spearl. See if I can find out what they did to Ki...our daughter. Don't worry, I'll hike before I let anybody sew wings on me."

"I didn't see any stitching on our daughter's back," I told her

"Figure of speech," she said. "Now let's go. Roth's getting away from us."

When we got to the "surgeons," Roth conversed with them for a while out of our earshot. Occasionally, he looked over at us. Finally, he waved us over. "This is Ishmael. He isn't the surgeon that fixed our friend, but he knows all about it."

"She's *much* better now," Ishmael told us. "Beside the wings, they fixed her metal problem, and removed most of her fear. I hear they did some unnecessary cosmetic work as well."

"Her metal problem?" Star asked.

"Yes, she was subject to becoming majick-starved, as you seem to be right now. They fixed her to draw metal through her feet. As long as she walks occasionally, she'll never have that problem again," Ishmael smiled.

"Could you do that for me?" Star asked.

"This Rover has given me permission to do all you require, but he doesn't order it. He's left it up to me. I believe you. I'm told your daughter has eyes this same color as yours."

"Then I'd like you to...fix my metal problem. If you will."

"And you?" Ishmael asked me.

"I'm good," I told him. I was about to question Star sternly about the soundness of this decision, when she looked at me and said, "I can't eat another bite of liver." I shut up.

I was told I couldn't watch the surgeons' secret majick, and Star said I should go with Roth. "He'll take you for a mug of mead."

As we were walking away, I saw one of the FireSprites touch a hand to Star's forehead. Then they gently laid her down on a bed of cotton.

Roth and I drank mead from a little keg set up by a fire. FireSprites were sitting here and there on the moss-covered ground. Some of them were loving. "Good mead," I told Roth as I noticed two girls and a boy in a highly passionate tangle. I smiled and said, "So, you think clothes are obscene."

"Wouldn't catch me walking around like that," he said, sipping his mead.

Before long, I saw Ishmael and another Sprite walking Star toward us. "Looks like she's done," Roth said.

As they got closer, I could tell that Star looked a bit groggy. Then I saw the wings.

"What happened?" I asked.

"She's just a little dazed by the majick. She'll wake fully in a few minutes," Ishmael told me. "She'll not starve again, as long as she walks once in a while. Her fear was small, but fought us and wouldn't be removed."

117

"And the *wings?*" I asked.

"This Rover gave us permission to do as we thought best. While we had her on the cotton, we fixed her properly, though did nothing cosmetic. Are you sure we can't help you, too?"

"No!" I said. "I'm definitely good. Now I think you better go one way and we, another, before she comes out of this daze."

Ishmael shrugged his wings and walked off. Roth said, "They should have glittered her skin and given her a glow. She makes a very pleasant FireSprite."

There was a little too much enthusiasm in his voice and smile. "She's not going to be in the mood," I told him.

XLI
A Fading Hallucination

Ilsa ventured out of her cave once a day, and always returned bearing little treats for us like strawberries and grapes. She made us a lovely nest of mint leaves, and watched through her glass whenever we loved in it. It seemed to make her happy, and Claireth thought it was cute. For some reason it seemed strange to me that I wasn't bothered by it, as if I should have been. But that was silly. Why would I be bothered by everyone being happy?

Even though she never stepped foot out of the cave, Claireth started feeling poorly. Her dust was gone, and her glittering skin faded. One night, after Ilsa cooked us a snail in herbs and sunflower oil, I told her we were going to have to leave. "I need to get her home," I said. "She can't live here very long."

Claireth was lying in our plush, mint bed, weak and sleepy. Ilsa examined her with her glass, and said, "I think my poor little hallucination's dyin'."

"Thank you for everything, Ilsa," I told her as I helped Claireth up and held her in my arms. "If I ever see Mother again, I'll tell her we met."

"Mother?" Ilsa asked. She seemed to be fading as quickly as Claireth.

"Star," I said. "My mother, Star."

Ilsa chuckled, then said, "Poor baby. Maybe I'll hallucinate *her* up."

"Good-bye," I said.

"Good-bye," Ilsa smiled. "Maybe when y'all gone, it'll mean my mind's a little less daft."

But we didn't go anywhere. I couldn't feel that crossing majick at all. "Oh, no!" I said aloud.

"Y'all still here," Ilsa smiled. "Guess I'm still daft."

Though I tried what seemed like every few minutes for hours and hours, I couldn't make that majick work. Couldn't even feel it. Claireth seemed weaker every time I stood her to try the majick again. Finally, Ilsa, looking at us through her glass, said, "Lie her down, child. Let her go in peace."

I eased Claireth onto the fragrant leaves, and combed her fine, pale hair with my fingers. "Can you hear me, sweetie?" I asked.

Through a weak smile, she whispered, "I've gone all raisin, Cutie Pie. Can I have a kiss?"

I touched my lips to hers, could feel my tears coming. Then she closed her eyes, and I sat watching my tears spark as they fell beside our bed.

XLII
Promised

I managed to keep Star walking west, and before long she seemed to be coming out of her fog. As she did, she folded herself into my arms and said, "Mmmm, I feel so good, Spearl. Love me."

We were just outside the little village, and Star, still drunk with Sprite majick, was becoming insistent. Her writhing against me was making our condition acute. "Do you think you could let us be alone for a bit," I asked Roth. Smiling, he fluttered away.

After a furious tussle, I was lying on my back with Star, exhausted and panting, on top of me. Then I looked up into the tree over us and saw Roth smiling down. "But they find clothes naughty," I said.

Then I heard Star say in my ear, "Love is the same everywhere. Love is lovely."

"How do you feel?" I asked.

"I feel very good," she said. "I'm not majick-starved or love-starved, though I wouldn't mind some water or wine. I'm thirsty."

"How does your back feel?"

"Now that you mention it, it itches. How about scratching for me...right between my shoulder blades."

"Right where your wings are?" I said.

Immediately, Star jumped up, just as Roth jumped down out of the tree and said, in a dreamy voice, "It was *beautiful*!"

"Was he watching the whole time?" Star grumbled as she reached around trying to feel what was on her back.

"Here," Roth told her. "If they're itching, I'll dust you." Then he threw something glittery on her and said, "Better?"

Suddenly, Star's wings began buzzing furiously, and a very startled look appeared on her face. "Dear Jess!" she exclaimed.

"You'll never get off the ground like that," Roth told her. "Relax! Don't buzz, *flutter*!"

Though Star had a notion to go back and kick some surgeon arse, I kept us moving west. "They're cute," I kept telling her, until she finally gave me a look that led to a prolonged silence.

After a while, Star seemed to cool a bit, and said, "At least I won't have to eat any more liver. I have to admit, this majick is very intriguing. I'd like to try and learn it."

"You can forget that," Roth told her. "They're very protective of that majick. They don't want the other HalfFire clans to have it."

"Why not?" Star asked.

"Still some old distrust from the day of the Glamour War."

"When did you have a war?" she asked him.

"Nobody remembers," he said. "Some say it was six thousand years ago."

"Long time to hold a grudge," Star said.

"And, anyway," Roth told her, "how are you going to learn that kind of majick when you can't even use your wings?"

"Why don't you teach me," Star said, surprising me.

"I will, if you'll Flutter with me," Roth said softly through a glowing blush.

"Get me off the ground," Star told him, "and I'll flutter with you till we turn blue."

"Ooooooh!" Roth cooed.

Our journey west was pleasant, and interrupted occasionally for Star's "lessons." Believe it or not, after just a couple such stops, she managed to get her feet off the ground.

"Up and down's easiest," Roth told her. Then, with his face blushing again, he said, "Follow me now, up high!"

Before long, I could no longer see them, and when they didn't return for a while, I became concerned. Finally, I saw them fluttering back to the ground, and Star looked suspiciously flushed and smiling. When I gave her a questioning look, she said, "Don't make promises around here unless you know what you're talking about. You'll be held to them."

XLIII
In Good Hands

Ilsa and I were weeping silently when the mouth of the cave lit up. Suddenly, my grief vanished, and I saw Ilsa smile. "I've hallucinated an angel," she said, "to take her home."

The Luminae gently scooped Claireth, mint bed and all, into her palms. "Why didn't you come sooner?" I asked.

"I'm afraid all weren't agreed about rescuing her twice. But I finally won the argument." Then she held her hands close to me and said through a beatific smile, "Climb in. I'll take you, too."

Once I was in Ariel's palms with Claireth, that wonderful being looked over at Ilsa and said, "Would you like to come, too, child? Your days here are spent."

"Am I still hallucinatin'?" she asked.

"Call it a vision," Ariel told her.

"Let's go," Ilsa said, standing out of her chair. "This cave gets chilly."

We arrived in our world just outside the cave entrance. "Where's Ilsa?" I asked.

"Gone to RealmWhite for a rest. Then she'll live another life...and another and another. Things take time."

In a moment or two, Claireth began stirring. Then she sat up and said, "You're so very beautiful!"

"Thank you," Ariel smiled.

"Yes. You, too," Claireth grinned.

"You must be more careful, little Sprites," Ariel told us. Then to me, she added, "You've still a bit of the aneke'lemental about you, and he won't stop yet."

Suddenly I recalled her touching my belly and saying, "Yes, I guess you'd better stay as you are."

"What am I?" I asked her.

"Moment to moment, you are what you are, what you become," she told me.

I thought about that for a bit, then asked, "Why couldn't I bring us back here? You said I didn't need the blue poison anymore."

"It was the cave," Ariel said. "It's full of metals, and you are, too. Your little feet work well at collecting them. But all that will fade soon. Still, you must be careful and hide for a time yet. He still seeks you."

I could tell she was about to leave, so I quickly asked, "Are Mother and Daddy here?"

Ariel laughed, a sound that made me want to weep with joy, and said, "You ask too much, precious Sprite! I'll be accused of meddling if I answer all your questions!"

Then she grew more brilliantly white. Just before she disappeared, I saw her smile and nod her head. Yes.

XLIV
Fair Play

We stopped, supposedly to sleep, in a tiny village just outside ClanFair. We wanted to be fresh when we arrived there and started our investigating. But Star and Roth wandered over to a group of Fairae girls, and came back with a mug of mead. "Take a drink," Star told me, and I did. Then she said, "Do you see that cute girl over there smiling at you. Well, she's going to take you behind that big oak. They know some *very* lovely techniques."

"Star!" I protested, but she was having none of it.

"Fair is fair, Spearl. And, anyway, you have no choice. You made a promise when you drank her mead. Call it a trade. And I want no more talk of Wanda May after this, or fantasizing about Lizabeth."

"I never..." I began, but she put her fingers on my lips, smiled wickedly, and said, "Go."

Her name was Lila, and that's all I'll say about my time behind the oak.

XLV
Wee Folk

My cute little lover was so angry with Prissi and Teali that, for a while, I had to Flutter with her several times a day to get her mind off it. It amazed me that loving her was always as wonderful as the first time.

Claireth felt sure that we were much safer now. "Rovers know our plight, and are keeping watch. They'll get word to us about which places to avoid and which ways to go. Rovers are fiercely loyal, and you and I have become their first charge. I also have them watching for Teali and Prissi. When I catch those two, and I will, they'll pay a high price for their betrayal."

"Why do you suppose they did it?" I asked her.

"He promised them something. I fear what it might be."

"Why? What do you think it was?"

"Fairae majick isn't as strong as ours. Their light is smaller and their dust less potent. And they haven't our knowledge. There are things they could do—things majick—if they knew how."

"Do you think he gave them new majick?"

"Whatever he gave, it won't be enough. If they fight my retribution when I catch them, it will come to fang and claw. I don't know any creature, pound for pound, who can defeat a First Rover in that arena."

"A First and a Fourth!" I said, folding into her sparkling arms.

Claireth and I traveled the realm, and she showed me many wonders. There were hollow trees to explore, little babbling falls of water, tiny spring ponds with enormous fish (which, of course, were minnows). We sat in eagles' nests high on craggy hills, and swam in this world's ocean (which felt just like that other world's). But I found it hard to call up my Naiadae there, and thought perhaps it was because we no longer needed them to arrive at amazing places of ecstasy. FireSprite LoveLock is an incredible bond, a love that interprets clues and sees through each other's eyes. And if you hurt one, you hurt both.

Whenever we swam, in pond or ocean, Claireth always spun us up to our three-foot size. The reason for this would be obvious to a fisherman, especially one who floats a fly on his line.

One summon, as we sat dripping in the sand by the sea, Claireth said, "Spinning is one of a HalfFire's strongest majicks. Now that your light grows fang and claw, I wonder if you can spin as well?"

"I don't know," I told her. "Could you teach me?"

"I can teach you Rover skills and tricks," she told me. "But I couldn't have taught your claws to come, or your fangs to grow in your pretty mouth."

"Do I look menacing with my fangs?" I asked with a grin.

"To an opponent," she said with exaggerated seriousness, "you are *terrifying*!" Then, with a giggle, she said softly, "But to me, they just make you extra cute."

"What about my claws?"

"Not cute at all," she said. "And I'd hate to run afoul of them."

After a little silent time, I said, "I worry a bit about *my* majick," I told her. "My Naiadae were sluggish when I tried to use them in the water."

"We don't need them," she said. Then she proved it to me, as we fluttered up, still big, toward the midsummon Inward Light.

Before we left the ocean—Rover Firsts were advising in the ether that we go south and west—Claireth wanted to see if I could spin myself down. "What do I do?" I asked her.

"That's like asking, how do I breathe, or how do I bear my fangs? One simply *does* at the appropriate moment."

"Well," I told her, "I know we spin left to grow, and right to go down."

"Really?" she said, smiling. "I'd never noticed. See, you know more than me. Try!"

I tried to remember how it felt to spin down. Nothing happened. But as soon as I let that thought go, I felt myself whirl, and was dragonfly size. "Ha!" I said, then spun myself right back up.

"You're amazing!" Claireth cried, grabbing me into a hug. "You really are a FireSprite, Cutie Pie, though I can't even imagine how the surgeons made it so! Even the false glow they gave you shines real. And look! Is that dust on your shoulders?"

"It's probably from you hugging me," I said. For some reason, I wasn't feeling as joyous as Claireth.

"I know my own dust!" she told me. Then, with her eyes gone shy, she said, "Please sprinkle me a bit."

Instead of trying my dust on my cutie pie love, I plopped down on my arse in the sand. "What's wrong?" Claireth asked.

"I'm not human anymore," I said, as she sat beside me.

Kissing my ear, she whispered, "That's what I've been telling you. Does it make you sad?"

I turned and looked at her intensely pretty and glowing face, fell into the depths of her ice-blue eyes, combed my fingers through her cornsilk-babysilk hair. How could I be sad? And I think, had I been human, the love I felt for her would have torn me to shreds, would have made it impossible for me to live without somehow crawling inside her and swallowing her whole at the same time. Yes! This love would be too much for a human. Suddenly, *finally*, I was glad and relieved to be done with that existence—done with that world. Still looking into Claireth's eyes, I smiled for her and grew my fangs just a tiny bit. "Oooooh," she cooed. "Are you my little tiger?"

"I'm your little FireSprite," I said in a husky purr. Then I loved her like a tiger.

Claireth had never eaten a fish from the sea, so I decided to call one before we left and bake it in Kelp. I called a brilliantly colored and glowing Dorado. Claireth was amazed. "How?" she asked as he flopped on the shingle.

"That's an easy trick," I told her. "A man once said that anyone touched by the wee folk could call a fish."

"Who are the wee folk?" she asked.

"Maybe they're us," I said. "Did the HalfFire ever live in the other world?"

"We used to cross back and forth, long ago, but we never stayed, never lived there." Then she thought for a moment and said, "If I'm a wee folk, do you think I could call out a fish?"

"Give it a try," I said as I was wrapping my Dorado in kelp.

I watched as Claireth stood facing the ocean, and I heard her mutter under her breath, "Come, fish, come."

All of a sudden, up and down the beach, fish came flying out of the water. There must have been fifty of them, all flouncing. "OH!" Claireth screamed, picking one up and throwing it back in the water. "Help me, Cutie Pie! Help me get them back in!"

Laughing to beat all helluva, Claireth and I ran up and down the beach, saving fish from the call of a wee folk.

Claireth loved the baked Dorado, so much so that she became a little toothy as she ate. "So *good*!" she said, smiling at me with those sharp little pearls gleaming.

Once finished with our fish, we sat, full and happy, in each other's arms. "My, but I'm stuffed," Claireth said, rubbing her tummy. "That was even better than the snail."

I dropped my head onto her shoulder, and after a bit, said, "I don't think it was the surgeons who changed me, Claireth."

"What do you mean, Cutie Pie?" she asked, rubbing *my* tummy now.

"Oh, they gave me wings, but I think it was Ariel that made me change."

After cogitating a bit, Claireth said, "I don't know about such things, but she's a very good Luminae. Don't you think so?"

"Yes, I do."

"She saved me twice, and you once. And she took the nice old lady to RealmWhite. That was a *very* good thing."

"It was," I agreed.

"So if she changed you, it must also be good—a *really good thing*."

"Sometimes, I still think about Daddy and Mother," I said.

"Do you miss them?" Claireth asked.

After thinking a moment, I said, "No. Not really. But sometimes I miss missing them."

"Perhaps we can go see them, if I can be sure it's safe."

"You know where they are?" I asked, surprised.

"Yes. They left ClanFair not long ago, heading west."

"Why didn't you tell me?" I asked.

"I just did!" she insisted.

"Sooner!" I said, jumping to my feet.

"They're careless, Cutie Pie, and it isn't safe. I've heard they sometimes forget and say your name. The fox may have spies watching them. Prissi and Teali were skulking around ClanFair while they were there. Rovers are keeping an eye on them, and will tell me when it's safe to take you to them."

I sat back down, and Claireth put her arm around me. "I'll take you when it's safe," she said again softly into my ear.

"It's not that I miss them," I told her, trying to arrange my thought. "But I feel I need to tell them, make them understand that I don't belong to them anymore. That their love for me must not be possessive, but become love for *my* love. Love for the fact that I've *found* love."

"Me!" Claireth chirped.

"Of course, you," I told her, pecking her cheek with a kiss.

"You will tell them some summon," she told me, "when it's safe. And it will be interesting to see how your mother looks with her new wings."

"*What?*"

"First Rover Roth has said she'd be a very fine FireSprite if the surgeons had given her a glow. Though he himself hasn't said it, there's rumor they've FlutterLoved."

"*Who* FlutterLoved?"

"Roth and Star," she said. "But it's not sure, so you didn't hear it from me!"

XLVI
Sketchy Information

Clanfair was a big village. As we entered it, Star and I drew curious looks. Even with her wings, Star didn't glow, and was a strange creature to the Fairae. But they were a friendly people, and before long we found some who were willing to tell us about "Jilhannah."

"She's a fearsome Rover," said a Fairae boy, who was also a Raptor—the Fairae version of Rovers, I suppose. "And she's quite a carouser! Drinks elderberry like spring water! I played in a LovePile with her and Claireth—her lover First. They're tigers, both, I can tell you. Gave me a little fang-bite, she did!" he laughed. "Best LovePile ever."

Other than finding out that our daughter was becoming a world class "carouser," we learned little other than that she and Claireth might be heading west. We'd hoped to get more to go on before we left, but we were becoming celebrities, and didn't like it. A lot of the Fairae, especially the Raptors, kept insisting that we attend their parties and drink their mead. Then they'd say, "Join our LovePile," and nod toward four or five Fairae tangled in a grope.

"Looks like fun," Star said to me once, grinning to beat all helluva.

"Let's go find our daughter," I told her.

Pursing her smile into an exaggerated pout, she said, "And you once called me parochial."

Just outside ClanFair, two Fairae girls came out of nowhere and started walking beside us. "Hello," Star said.

"Hi!" one of them answered.

Then the other spoke. "Is it true you seek the one they call Jilhannah, but who *isn't* Jilhannah?" she said conspiratorially.

"Yes!" Star said, hope rising in her eyes.

"We know where she is," the girl told her, casting about anxiously. "She's hiding in a cave with her Rover lover."

"Could you take us there?" Star asked.

Both the Fairae girls were looking around nervously now, as if they were afraid someone might be watching them. "We've never been," one of them said. "But we're told it's west, past a valley with many flower-fields. In the hills past the valley, you'll find the cave."

"That's not much to go on," Star told her.

"It is what it is," the girl said, totally distracted now and looking about at the sky. "Let's get out of here, Teali," she said. "I think they're back." Then they buzzed away, quick as a flash.

"Well!" Star said, hands on her hips. "What did you make of that?"

"I don't know," I told her. "Do you trust those two?"

"Not a bit," she said. "But we're going west anyway, though I don't think there's much chance of finding a specific cave by those directions."

"I know," I told her. "'In the hills past the valley' isn't much of a clue."

Star cogitated a moment, then said, "There are hills past the valley of Tara."

"If this was our world," I said, "that would seem to be where we're heading."

"I wish Roth hadn't wandered off," Star said. "Now that we're past the villages, I'd like to be big again."

No sooner had she spoken than Roth fluttered down beside us. "Wanna be big?" he smiled.

"We do," Star told him.

"Might cost you a Flutter," he said, blushing like a glowing beet.

"I don't sell my love for favors," Star told him through a wicked grin. "But I'd love a little kiss," she said, leaning in with a Naiadae smooch.

That seemed to suffice, and Roth spun us all up to three feet tall. "All-the-way big," I told him.

"The Lady won't be able to fly if I grow her so," he told me with a frown.

"Flying might come in handy, Spearl. This will do," Star said.

"Well *I* don't have any wings. Make *me* normal size," I insisted. In an instant, Roth did. Looking down at Star, I said, "You're so *cute!*"

"And you're too big," she said, fluttering up to give me a kiss.

"You're going to be on your own for a while," Roth told us. "We Rovers are very busy watching over Claireth and Jilhannah. Keeping them safe."

"You know where they are?" Star said, incredulity loud in her voice.

"For the most part," Roth said matter-of-factly.

"Where?" Star insisted. "Why haven't you told us? Why do you help us look for them if you already know where they are?"

"I do what I can," Roth told her. "Claireth and Jilhannah are FireSprite Rovers, and in terrible danger. We'll give them away to *no one*! Especially aliens."

"So your help has all been false," Star said angrily.

"Never," Roth insisted. "I've kept you from harm, though you don't know it. You have wings now, and are no longer majick-starved. If you are to find Jilhannah, the Universe will sanction it." Then he said with a saddened face, "You seem ungrateful, and it hurts me, little FlutterLove."

"I'm sorry," Star said, obviously moved by his sadness. Then she kissed him again, and said, "Thank you for all your help, and for loving me so."

Roth smiled and said, "One more thing. Those two wretched Fairae you were talking to are *not* friends. Listen to nothing they say. They'll be dealt with soon enough."

"Who are they?" I asked.

"Betrayers."

"They told us Claireth and Jilhannah are in a cave," Star told him.

"Then, for some reason, they want *you* in a cave. Trust me, my First and her lover are safe, and not in a cave."

"Are they somewhere west?" Star smiled.

"They're somewhere," Roth smiled back. Then he spun down tiny and was gone.

XLVII
Rat Trap

When we recovered from our feast of fish, I said to Claireth, "Maybe we should get moving—go where the Rovers said we should. Southwest, wasn't it?"

"Yes," she said with a cute little burp.

"We could go to my old home place—swim in the pond."

"Already thought of that," she said, and I suddenly noticed her glow was strong and blushing red. "But I have something for you first, something I've saved. Something for only the intensely LoveLocked," she grinned.

"What?" I said, and her blush made me blush.

"Just lie back and stay big while I spin down," she said. "You'll see."

Claireth spun down as I lay back in the sand and closed my eyes. It startled me at first, and my eyes popped open wide. "OH!" I cried. Then it became incredible, and I was all a-flutter with love for the seriously LoveLocked.

After our something wonderful, Claireth and I headed toward what, in another world and an increasingly distant memory, had been my home. Claireth wanted us to stay big a while and walk. "For your metals," she told me.

Then I realized, and said, "I don't need them anymore! My feet are just feet—just FireSprite feet!"

"Then I'll worry about that no longer!" she smiled. "One less thing. Now let's go to the pond over the ridge. Rovers are going to meet us there. They've baited a trap with a fox of their own—a FireFriend who we once helped when a log rolled onto him."

"A trap for those two scoundrel Fairae?" I asked, my face pinched angrily.

"They think they're coming to spy, but they're coming for my ire. When it's time, I'll teach you a new trick—deep FireSprite majick that's rarely used."

"Not fang and claw?" I asked.

"Not unless they insist," she told me.

Every once in a while, as we made our way to the southwest, a Rover would drop down and briefly join us. After introducing me, Claireth would go off with the Rover and talk privately. When this had happened twice, I asked her, "Are you keeping something secret from me?"

"Yes," she said, as if that were normal and natural.

"Well, I don't like it!" I said with my hands on my hips.

Claireth laughed so hard that she folded her wings and rolled on the ground. Finally, she stopped long enough to say, "You look so *funny* when you do that!"

I tried something else. Through a terrible pout, I said, "It hurts my feelings."

Claireth came to me, gave me a hug, and said, "No it doesn't. You're just nosey. And it isn't really secrets, just First Rover business. As a Fourth, you can't expect to be let in on *everything*."

"But what about as your LoveLocked Cutie Pie?" I asked, my pout gone poutier.

Claireth pretty much folded, and said, "I'll tell my Cutie Pie anything she wants to know."

"What's the plan?" I smiled, thinking there might still be a *little* human girl left in me.

"We're bait," Claireth told me. "Our FireFriend fox told Prissi and Teali how to find the pond, and that he wanted them to go there and keep an eye out for us. You and I are to get in the water and splash around a bit. When I get a signal, we'll FlutterLove just over the pond. Fairae don't know how to love like that, and won't be able to resist watching. While they are, my Rovers will surround them, seven in all not counting you and me. Four of them are Firsts. Those two won't escape all that fang and claw."

"But...but...do you think we should do that?" I said.

"Do what?" she asked.

"Use our loving for *bait!*"

Claireth giggled and said, "I won't mind doing it."

"I don't know if I *want* our love to be used that way," I told her. "Our love is a *good* thing."

"Catching those two will be good," she countered.

"I just don't know," I said.

"It's okay, Cutie Pie. If you don't want to, I'll get Rover Ellannah to do it with me. She has hair something like yours. They'll never know the difference."

"Ellannah?" I asked. "Isn't that your favorite FireSprite name?"

"Yes," she said. "I love it almost as much as your cutie pie name."

"And you'll Flutter with her instead of me?" I whined.

"Oh, no," she smiled. "I'm going to Flutter with *you*!"

"Good!" I said, though I wondered later if Claireth had a little bit of human girl, too.

XLVIII
Tailed

Before I became truly HalfFire, summon and night seemed pretty much the same to me. Now I could see the difference. Things glowed differently at night. It was subtler and softer. During summon, the glow is crisper, in sharper focus.

On the night we sprung our trap, the invisible moon was over us. Though I still couldn't see it, I was very aware of its presence, and stared for a bit at the circle of dark where it blocked the stars. Claireth and I were already big, and in the water. We splashed and giggled and kissed and petted, and before long I forgot about the trap. Then Claireth's eyes got that look in them that tells me I'm about to get something I'll like. "Flutter," she whispered in my ear.

Usually we Fluttered up high, but doing it just over the pond turned out to be even better. We had a lovely view of ourselves reflected in the water. "Oh, we should have thought of this sooner!" I said through my sighs.

"Necessity bears invention," Claireth said. I was way caught up in our Flutter, and had no idea what she meant. Then, just off to the north of the pond, a Rover shouted, "We've got them!"

That didn't register either, and by the time we finally ceased our love, we heard a good bit of giggling from the bank of the pond. Through heavy breaths, Claireth said, "Do you have them?"

One of the Rovers—and it may have been Ellannah—giggled and said, "We got them, First Rover Claireth. Good job!"

However much the fox had enhanced their majick, it was of no use to Prissi and Teali against nine Rovers. The Fairae were each made to face the opposite side of a small tree, with their arms reached around it and their hands tied together. Claireth and the other Firsts went off and discussed for a bit. After reaching some kind of consensus, they returned and Claireth said to the captive Fairae, "We've decided to mark you. Every HalfFire will learn of the mark, and you'll be shunned. If you go to a village, they'll chase you out. None will love you." Then she walked up behind Prissi, laid her fingers on the small of the Fairae's back and said, "Oh yes. This will hurt a bit."

Prissi screamed as a line of light extended from the base of her spine. Then it solidified into a long, red bushy tail. Teali was next, and she wailed terribly as her tail was pinned on. Then the Rovers released the now tailed captives, and Claireth said, "Those can never be removed without paralyzing you. If you lie down with foxes, you get up with tails."

While we Rovers prepared to depart, Claireth said to the fox-tailed Fairae, "Stay here at this pond until drawn. Disobey at your peril. Any more crimes by you two will demand fang and claw."

As we flew away, she said to me, "That was *fun*! We should find another pond!"

XLIX
Ghosted

"Now what?" I said, our escort gone to join his Rovers.

"I say we head toward those hills the Fairae girls told us about," Star said.

"But Roth seemed to think that might be a trap."

"Exactly," Star told me. "If that fox is looking for us, we'll just let him find us. I told you I'd protect Kimikin, and I will."

"You've said her name again!"

"Kimikin, Kimikin, Kimikin," she said through a gnarly grin.

"Remember," I told her, "you don't have any majick."

"Oh, I've plenty of majick! It's just a little tied up right now. But if I stop plugging the conduit, it will all be available."

"Wouldn't we get sucked back to our world?" I asked.

"Yes, but we'd have at least a few minutes, long enough, I think, to skin a fox."

"Sounds like a plan," I said. "But I'd still prefer to search for our daughter."

"If we eliminate the threat to her and Claireth, I'm sure Roth will take us to them. I could feel him wanting to before he left, but he's a fiercely loyal Rover."

"You were in his thought?" I asked.

"I was in his *feel*," she said with a strange look.

"I think he has a crush on you," I told her.

"Yes," Star said, and I wondered if she'd felt that, too.

As we made our way west, Star practiced her flying. "It was easier when I was tiny," she told me. "But I'm getting the hang of it. I might just keep these."

"You'd have to stay three feet tall to use them," I told her.

"That's true, I can't spin," she said. "I wonder if those surgeons could fix *that*."

"You're kidding, right?" I asked.

"I might be," she said, fluttering up to kiss my nose. "You're so *big*!" she said, dropping back to the ground. "You'd be much nicer as a little cutie pie."

"This is the Tara Valley," Star said as we looked down onto fields of gently glowing wildflowers. "See there," she said. "I used to have a house in those hills."

"Not funny," I told her.

"If we forget the past..." she said.

When she didn't finish, I asked, "If we forget the past, what?"

"It'll come back around and bite you in the arse," she said, fluttering herself behind me, which made me turn quickly.

"None of that," I told her. "There are probably a number of caves in those hills. But are we looking for one big enough for the size you are now, or for Sprites gone tiny?"

"Either way, we've got a fart's chance in a hurrikin party of finding it. I'm more interested in finding that fox." Then she looked out over the valley and hollered, "Kimikin!"

We made our way down into the village-less valley, and were both enthralled by the glowing flower-fields. "Not a lectric farm in sight," Star said, "yet it glows magnificently. That stand of violets over there reminds me of my old Dark Star."

"Not getting nostalgic for those days, are you?" I asked.

"Even though my mind was a mess, Spearl, when I began Star City, my motives were sincere. I did love those people, just as I loved them when you and I returned there."

I couldn't help thinking that the love she wanted in return, back in Star City, left her bloody. "I'm sorry I couldn't help you..." I began, but couldn't say it.

"...stay sane," she finished for me.

I was just recognizing that plain where Mother and Star faced off— where I was put to sleep and the Fierae took my sister from World— when I saw those eyes. Star saw them, too. "We've been looking for you," Star said to the fox.

"Come with me, and I'll no longer need your daughter," he told Star.

"Come with you where? Why?"

"To my demesne—a place I've isolated here in the BorderRealm. It's time to prepare for the thousand years' end. I need a queen to learn from and to teach. I need an aneke'lemental, and I only need one. It will be you, or it will be Kimikin."

I could see Star's eyes flicker to flame, and her skin was starting to glow. Then the fox spoke again, and he actually wore a wicked smile. "Yes!" he said. "Fire! One of the tricks I desire."

"I'm about to show it to you!" Star told him, her voice gone elemental.

"Star," I said. "The Conduit! Are you still..."

"It won't draw us back for a minute or two," she said. "Long enough to barbecue one insignificant animal."

As soon as she said that, I saw *two* foxes. Then four, eight, and on and on until we were completely encircled by them. "How much fire do you have?" they all said at once through hideous grins.

"Spearl!" Star cried. "Cocoon! Go up! Now!"

I could see her skin beginning to flow molten, and lectrics slammed into the ground from her fingers. She didn't have to tell me twice. In a moment I was high above that place, that two-time battlefield.

It came from Star like the sun rising out of a hole. Nearly a klick all around her flared to scalding mist, and I could have sworn I heard the flowers themselves scream. As high as I was above her, the shock of her blast battered my cocoon, and I feared I'd lose the attention of my Zephrae.

But somehow it held together. When the vapor of her cataclysm cleared, I could see Star below me, down on one knee with her chin dropped onto her chest. Her skin was still molten, and I saw that she no longer had wings. But as her fire settled, those delicate, gossamer appendages reformed, glowing on her back. With a little flash, her inferno faded, and she once again wore her caramel skin instead of a lava flow. I dropped down beside her and tried to help her stand, but I couldn't touch her. I was becoming a ghost. "The conduit!" I cried, but she didn't seem to hear.

I didn't know how the surgeons' majick worked to keep Star from becoming majick-starved, but I doubted they'd expected it to have to compensate for this kind of release. I was fading fast, and so was the pack I was holding. I pitched it onto the ground in front of Star and said, "Inside it! The livers I caught for you!"

Though she still didn't seem to hear, her hand did move. She touched my pack and it solidified again. She opened it and began to eat. "Trying," she muttered, blood dripping down her chin.

I still looked and felt faded, but I didn't fall back to our world. I could see that Star was crying, trying to swallow huge chunks of the Naiadae chilled liver. Then she stood and said in a choking voice. "Walk with me. I have to get off this scorched earth—get my feet on clean ground. The conduit is plugged, but I need my strength to keep it that way."

"Why am I still a ghost?" I asked her.

"Don't know," she groaned, staggering away from the devastation she'd wrought. "Can barely hear you."

At the same time, on a little plain just outside the village of Ilsa, a ghost appeared. "Now what?" he said.

Being in two places at once is bad enough, but being solid in neither is a world class pain in the arse. Somehow, as I looked east toward Ilsa, I knew everything that other ghost knew in the other world. I suspected he was aware of me as well.

Wanting to assess my assets, I called lines and they appeared. But my ghost hands wouldn't rest on them. I could also call a Zephre cocoon, but when it rose it lifted without me. I was a phantasm the elementals could hear but not touch. Feeling just a little bit gollammed, I sat and realized I couldn't even feel my arse on the ground.

"I'm a ghost in our world, too," I told Star, who was leaning against a small oak, still trying, and mostly failing, to eat cold, raw liver.

"I can let the conduit open long enough for you to be pulled completely through to our world."

"No!" I told her. "Bring me back here!"

"Can't," she said.

"Then come with me. We'll find more blue poison and come back."

"Not leaving Kimikin," she said. "Going to send you back."

"Don't you dare, Star!" I screamed. "By our love, by all we've been through, by all we've shared from Mother's womb to that fragrant tomb we rose from, *don't do it*!"

She looked at me through a terrible sadness, and I wasn't sure what she would do. "Please!" I begged.

142

In this world, *our* World, I knew I was arguing with Star not to be sent back here. But *this* part of me wished she would. I wanted to be whole so I could *do* something. Talk about being of two minds. Then I saw someone coming, riding a muley out of Ilsa.

Star and I were known in that village. In fact, we'd given it its name. Kimikin had even been there as a baby, though I'm sure she doesn't remember it. Back then, when Star returned, she still wanted to help the people of her once Star City. I've often wondered if, unbeknownst to me, she'd given them the wind and waterwheel teck.

It was a man on the muley. He wore a long, light coat, onto which was pinned a silver badge in the shape of a windmill's hub and blades (I, of course, having thrown Star my pack, was still naked). When he was about thirty meters from me, he stopped. "Shite!" he said. "You're a ghost!"

Turning his muley faster than muleys will usually turn, he started making tracks back toward Ilsa. But I called to the Terrae, and held his muley's hoofs fast to the ground. I could see its hind muscles wanting to kick. "Git up! Git up!" the man kept insisting, but I had his muley firmly anchored.

"I'm not a ghost," I said as I walked up beside him. "I'm an Apprentice, and I'm caught between two worlds!"

"Ain't that what a ghost *is*?" he shouted at me, still flicking his muley's reigns.

"Look at me," I told him. "My name is Spearl. What's yours?"

Giving up on getting his muley going, he looked down at me and said, "Mistuh Spearl? I'm Junior. Junior Thomas. Y'all used to come see me and Mama when I was just a chap. Tol' stories 'bout my grandaddy and Tara. How'd you git all ghostified?"

Being torn between two worlds is a tiring condition, and I could tell sleep would take me soon, like it or not, in both worlds. "It's a long story, Junior, but I do remember you and your mama. Do you still have that lectric globe from old Star City?"

Junior Thomas smiled and said, "Still do, but I don't never use it. Different kinda lectrics we git outa the wheels and mills. Don't know all that stuff, though. I ain't no teck. I'm constable, now. I know you ain't been 'round here most of a dozen years, but Ilsa's a fine place, kinda place you and the rised-up lady used to talk about."

"I'm going to have to sleep, Junior. I'd just as soon not do it out on this plain."

"Always a bed for you at Mama's, Mistuh Spearl, ghostified or not. But ain't you got some ghostly clothes you could put on? Bad enough lookin' through you without looking through all your parts."

"Afraid not," I told him. "I left my ghost clothes in the other world."

"Can ghosts ride muley's?" he asked.

"I can sit on the ground," I told him. "Hopefully I can sit on a muley as well."

"Here," he said, removing his long coat. "Wear this."

"Junior pitched me his coat, and I had it in my hands for a second. But slowly it made its way through me and to the ground. I managed to pick it up long enough to hand it back to him. Though I couldn't feel the muley when I climbed on, I stayed put and said, "Guess I'm stuck with FireSprite customs."

"Means stuck naked, don't it?" he said.

"That's what it means," I told him.

"I'll circle us 'round and come up behind the house. Don't know which would scare people more, bein' ghost or bein' naked. Guess we're saddled with both."

I smiled, as our taboos about nudity suddenly seemed more foolish to me than FireSprite strictures on clothes.

"I need to sleep, Spearl," Star told me, obviously decided against sending me back.

"Me, too," I told her.

Propping herself against the tree, she sat with her feet flat on the ground. "I can feel the surgeon majick working. My feet will feed me while I rest."

"Do you think you'll be able to bring me back?"

"The corridor flows in one direction, Spearl. I can *send* you, but I can't *bring* you."

"Then sleep," I told her. "It's all I can do to keep my eyes open. Two places at once is draining."

"It'll get worse," she told me. "You'll get hungry." Then she fell away into sleep.

L
Wonderful Times and Disturbing News

With those nemesis Fairae girls tailed and shamed, Claireth and I felt a little bit safer from the fox. "Two less spies, I think," Claireth told me. "They won't risk being torn, and their whereabouts will be pretty obvious with them wearing those bright red, foxy tails."

"In my world, foxy means pretty," I told her.

"They're still pretty," she giggled, "if you don't look behind."

"But they were *never* cutie pies," I said.

"Not ever," she agreed.

"Do you still know where Mother and Daddy are?" I asked.

"No, but now that we're done tracking down those two little bitches, I can free up some Rovers to find them again. Still, I won't take you to them till I know it's safe. I'd do *anything* for you, Cutie Pie, except put you in danger. So please don't ask it of me. It hurts me so to say no to you."

"Then say yes to this," I told her. "Why don't you spin up big, lie down and relax, and I'll stay down here and show you how seriously LoveLocked I am."

With her eyes wide, and her fangs just a touch tweaked in her grin, she said, "You really want to?"

"I really, really do," I said.

Life with Claireth was wonderful. There were times, back in that other world, when I thought I'd known joy, but I hadn't. Not even close. Now I experienced it moment to moment, and when I loved with Claireth it became something that will never be named, never be written about, never understood.

I was no longer sure why Mother and Daddy had returned to this world. My mind told me it was to take me home, to make me human again. But that seemed so nonsensical, so insane, that I couldn't even consider it. Maybe they'd just come to pay a visit. Then I thought about Mother with wings, and giggled. "And she wanted me to go around clothed!" I thought.

145

"Where shall we fly to now?" Claireth asked me one night, her delicate fingers playing in my hair.

"Let's find a pond and Flutter over it," I said. "Or let's flutter to the moon and light it up with our glow."

"It's a long way!" Claireth said, touching my nose. "The air gets too thin to breathe."

"I was just kidding," I told her.

"I know!" she chirped. "I was kidding back. But it's true that the air gets thin. I've been high as you can go, where the stars are so bright you can taste them."

"I want to see," I told her.

"Let's go!" she said.

Up and up we flew into that lovely night air. From the barely breathable height, all the world's glows melded together. Only the shine of the sea looked different. The Stars were so big and bright I wanted to stick out my tongue and lick them. After a while, Claireth said to me, "Stop flying, now. Tuck away your wings and let's fall together. After a moment it will feel like floating, and I'll kiss you sweetly all the way to the ground."

"Won't we go *splat*?" I asked her, imagining myself caught up in her love as the world came up fast to kiss us!

But Claireth giggled and said, "Our wings would never let that happen, Cutie Pie. It's like breathing, you know. In the end, we'll flutter, all dusty with love!"

Held in each other's arms, we floated down like dandelion fluff. When our wings finally opened, the dust coming off them made me smile.

One night, at a little pond we'd found, Claireth's eyes went distant the way they did when she read the ether. Once they focused again, she seemed to be cogitating. "What is it?" I asked her.

"Something has happened," she said.

"What?" I asked.

"I'm not sure," she told me. "It seems nobody is."

"Nobody's sure of *what*?" I tried again.

"There's a big, round circle northwest of ClanFair, black and burned. There are rumors that patches of sand there have turned to glass. The Fairae say a flash was seen as far as the villages east of ClanFair."

"Has anyone seen Mother and Daddy?"

"No."

"Maybe we should go there."

"We'll learn nothing that I can't hear from my Rovers, though I do want to go a little more north so I can hear better. A lot of them have gone up there to investigate."

I must have looked worried, because Claireth began stroking my hair and purring. But it was a different kind of worried. Call it worry without fear. "How far north should we go?" I asked.

"Let's go to the ocean, north of where you fed me fish."

"And feed you *more* fish?" I smiled, brushing her cornsilk away from her eyes.

"Maybe you can teach me to call out just one!" she giggled.

"Why?" I laughed. "It was *fun* throwing them all back in!"

LI
Aneke'lemental Trap

"What made you come out here?" I asked Junior as we rode toward Ilsa.

"Saw a flash," he said. "Looked like a giant mirror catching the sun for a moment. That what ghostified you, that flash?"

"In a way," I told him.

Somehow he managed to get me into the house without anyone seeing the naked ghost riding with him on his muley. I was so tired, I barely made it in and to his bed. "Sleep in here," he said. "My room. Mama's nappin'. She's old old now, Mistuh Spearl, so don't let her see you. Scare sheet right out her, I'm sure."

"Thank you, Junior," I said.

"You're welcome, Mistuh Spearl. Don't know what ghosts eat, but you get hungry, let me know."

I sat against the tree with Star, though I couldn't feel it on my back. Sleep fell over me like a heavy blanket. But, somehow, I was still aware, could hear Star breathing, could even see her sitting there with her feet planted on the ground. At the same time, I was very much asleep. I doubt if I could have willed myself to spit.

Then I saw the child. It was a little human girl, maybe nine years old, dressed in a ragged, sack of a dress. She walked up to Star, bent toward her, and said, "Wake up, Lady! Come save us from the fox!"

Now I really wanted to wake up, but it wasn't happening. Star, however, roused and said, "Oh! Who are you?"

"I'm called Shine. I've escaped, but my sisters are captive still—twelve in all. We saw a flash, and the barrier that holds us in the cave weakened. I managed to slip through, but my sisters are still inside. If he finds me gone, he'll punish them with his whip." Then the little girl turned around and lifted her ragged dress. Her back and bottom and legs were scarred with lacerations—some old, some still raw.

I could see the tears falling from Star's angry eyes. "I've killed that bastard!" she said. "Why did he keep you in a cave?"

"He stole us and brought us to this land of night. He says we're all Apprentice girls, and he wants our majick. But if we *are*, our majick hasn't come yet, and may not come for years. Please don't let him keep us that long," she wept.

Star hugged the little girl to her—they were about the same size—and said, "He's gone! Now take me to this cave and I'll set your sisters free."

Something wasn't right. This little girl's name was Shine, and she knew what it was like to be whipped. So had my sister Starshine, very near this place so long ago. "Wake up! Wake up! Wake up!" I insisted, but I simply could not, as Star and little Shine walked out of my circle of awareness.

LII
Light of my Life

Being very careful, Claireth only called out a dozen fish. I chose a nice Dorado, then helped her throw the others back in. Thanking the beautiful fish for his flesh, I scooted his light away, and gathered kelp. "Find me some onions, pretty fisher-girl," I said to Claireth. "And grapes, if you see some!"

"Mmmm! I love your fish!" she squealed as she flew off in a flash.

When she was gone, I looked out over the ocean. Before she appeared, I knew she would by the peaceful feeling that washed over me. Her light was brilliant as she walked over the sea to where I sat on the beach. "Hello, Ariel," I sighed.

Claireth returned with the onions, and said, "What happened? You look like somebody flew in and loved you while I was gone."

I smiled up at her with Ariel's peace still soaking me. "She walked," I said. "Over the ocean."

Claireth plopped down beside me and hugged me to her. "I can feel it, now, coming off you. The Luminae Lady came, didn't she?"

"Yes."

"Why do I feel like you're keeping a secret from me?" she asked.

"I'd never keep secrets from such a cutie pie love as you," I told her. "I have to go to Mother. I'm going to be bait again."

"*We!*" she said. "*We* will be bait."

"I have to go someplace where you can't go. But only for a very short time."

"No, no, no!" Claireth insisted, her tears sparking in the sand.

I could feel her sadness so acutely that I grabbed her into a fierce embrace and made her feel my peace. "See," I whispered, hearing her weeping cease. "Ariel will be with me the entire time. She knows you're the dearest thing to me, and has sworn to bring me back to you." That last part wasn't exactly true. But it was a very tiny lie to make my darling rest easy, and I wasn't ashamed.

"Tell me the plan," Claireth smiled.

LIII
Cotched

Waking was traumatic. One minute my awareness was in a circle around me, the next, I was in a bed in a house in Ilsa. Then I was sitting against that tree, looking at the place where Star had been.

Fortune had me find a torn scrap of the little girl's dress on a bush, and I knew I was on their trail when I saw their shuffled footprints. Before long, I came to the hills. They were as aglow as everything else, except for a yawning mouth in the hillside. I started climbing toward it.

With a flash of the other world in my head, I awoke on Junior's bed. I peeked out his bedroom door into the kitchen, where he and his mother were sitting. Her back was to me. "It's okay, Mistuh Spearl. I 'splained to Mama that you been ghostified. She's okay."

"Come on in, Spearl," she said, turning to me. "I'll be a ghost, too, soon. Figure the Universe gettin' me used to the idea."

"That isn't the way of it, Clara Thomas," I told her. "But you're a brave soul, and will come back strong." Then, to Junior I said, "Do you know of a cave in the hills?"

"There's said to be a cave where an old witch lives. Sometimes kids go up there on a dare and come back with stories."

"Some says it's Ilsa, still pinin' for Star," Clara said.

"It ain't Ilsa, Mama. That's just old grandmother tales."

"Didn't say it was true!" Clara Thomas snapped at Junior. "I said, *some says*."

"Do you know where it is?" I asked Junior.

"About," he said.

"Then let's go. If I can ride a muley, I can ride on your back. And *you* are going to ride the lines."

There was nothing I could do about Junior's hands, but the ride across the plain would be so brief it wouldn't matter. He was in for the ride of his life. "I sure hope nobody sees you butt naked and piggy backin'," Junior said as I called lines.

"They'll think you're an Apprentice," I smiled. "Now don't

get scared and drop off. We're going to go fast."

Junior tensed at first, but then he relaxed and started whooping. "Yee ha!" he shouted. "We flat out flyin'!"

When we arrived at the hills, I slowed us and dropped the lines. Then I told Junior to show me his palms. There was a touch of redness. "You make Clara feed you liver tonight," I told him. "And spinach."

"Now what?" he asked.

"Go home and eat liver!" I answered.

"Had a feelin' I'd be walkin' back," he said.

"I'll come visit when all this is straightened out, Junior. I promise. And I'll tell you tales like you've never heard."

"Don't know, Mistuh Spearl, you tol' me some whoppers when I was a chap."

"You ain't heard nothing, yet," I said.

As he started walking back toward Ilsa, I heard him say, "What about *this* gollam tale!"

I saw neither human girls, nor Star at the cave entrance. If there was a barrier of some sort, it had no effect on me. Inside, the walls of the cave glowed softly. I walked for a ways, then saw Star staring down at something. As I got closer, I saw his glowing eyes.

Star and the fox didn't seem to be aware of me yet, and I heard her say, "I won't go anywhere with you, and I'm about to burn you again."

"Probably not," he said. "You're already drained from that last little show, and I've heard from two lovely spies that this cave is full of metals that stifle elemental majick. You won't breach my barrier at the entrance, either. I can keep you here till you die of loneliness—unable to majick, unable to save your daughter. If you won't come with me, she will."

"She *won't*!" Star told him. "Nor will I!"

Then the fox looked right at me and said, "Ah! Here's some incentive, now. Seems he's gotten himself half in and half out—half out and half in. In his current condition, I can take him anywhere I like. So if you won't go, I'll show him my demesne. I'll show him my ability to inspire despair. It's an amazing torment that will follow him even into sleep."

As soon as he stopped speaking, Star cried out, "I'm sending you back, Spearl! I love you!"

There was a little pop that I felt in my ears, and suddenly I was whole again, standing there with Star and that infernal creature. "That shouldn't have happened," he said. "No matter. Stay here and think for a while," he told Star. "But if you both fall asleep, I'll tear out his throat."

"Who *are* you?" Star growled.

"You can call me Loose," he said. "Call out that name when you're ready to come to me. Otherwise, stay here as my guest. I may even feed you, though time sometimes gets away from me, so who knows. Now I'm off to find little Kimikin, or at least find a way to let her know I've my tongue on her parents' throats. If you decide to avoid all that and come with me, just call." Then he was gone.

LIV
Lovely Waiting

"So where do we go to meet Ariel?" Claireth asked me, her toothy mouth full of fish.

"We stay here," I told her. "Ariel said she'd come for me when it's time."

"But where do I go? How long will you be gone? It will hurt to be without you. They say a LoveLocked Sprite will tear herself if her love is taken away."

I snuggled up next to her, put my hand on her belly, and said, "You're our babe's house. You must *never* tear it."

"No," she said. "But she swore to bring you back, right?"

"She did," I lied. "Now stop fretting and eat, or you'll make me think you don't like my fish anymore."

"Let's call some out later and throw them back in," she smiled. "Then we'll Flutter over the sea, and make them jealous of our love."

After we ate, we swam. Then we sat in the sand, still big, but nonetheless like cuddlebugs. Claireth was quiet, and I said to her, "It could be some time till she comes for me. What shall we do while we're waiting?"

"The things we do," she smiled. Then she put her hand on my belly and said, "It's started growing. Maybe I'll sit here and watch your belly rise."

"You won't be far behind me," I said. "We'll be fat little grapes together."

"Then we'll go to BornHome, and they'll take such lovely care of us. They'll bring us berries and cool flower-water, and big chunks of pecans to munch. When the time comes, they'll hold us down and sprinkle a little dust to make the pain bearable. Then we'll push out our babes, and drink elderberry to make us rest."

"I know it will hurt," I told her. "But in a way, it's sad I can only do it once."

"You can do it as many times as you want," Claireth said.

"I thought you told me only once!"

155

"You and I can spark one babe each, and then no other sparks will fly from us. If you want another, you have to do it the messy way."

"With *who*?" I asked.

"I know some Raptors that would love to oblige you," she giggled.

"But I don't *like* it," I told her.

"You're a tiger when you're full of elderberry," she said. "And you don't seem to mind so much then."

"I really don't remember that LovePile," I told her.

"There's Raptors who do, and some of them are boys," she said through a wicked grin.

"Are *you* going to do it to get another babe?" I asked her.

"I haven't even birthed this one yet, Cutie Pie, and you're already wanting me done up again?"

"Would you?" I persisted. "Might you?"

"I only would if we were to LovePile together again. Since you said you never will, I think I'll be stopped at one babe."

"I never said I wouldn't," I told her. "I said I wouldn't get drunk again. But now that I know all these things, I *might* get that drunk again."

Claireth giggled and said, "You're so fickle. I'm glad I'm not a boy."

"Why?" I asked.

"Well, first because you like girls, which was lucky for me, and second because if I was a boy, you'd come around for one squirt, then I'd never see you again. Think of the hearts that will break," she said, throwing her hand over her heart and falling back into the sand.

"Ha!" I told her. "You'll be lucky to plant your one squirt, little Rover boy."

Laughing to beat all helluva, Claireth found a big stick of driftwood, and held it in front of her like an enormous boy part. "Come let me in, little FireSprites girl," she said in a husky voice. "I'll give you a squirt and a babe."

"It's too big!" I squealed.

"I'll just give you half," she said, and we fell into the sand roaring laughter.

LV
Surrender

When the fox was gone, Star said, "How did you get back here?"

"If you don't know, I sure don't," I told her. "What did you do?"

"I released my block on the corridor. You should have been sucked back home. Maybe if your other self was very close to you... but I don't know."

"Are you blocking it now?" I asked.

"I can't find it at all, Spearl."

"What does that mean?"

"It means I'm not sure how to get back. I'll have to figure it out, a majick that will work from this side. The other times we went back we were sucked through."

"So," I said. "It's complicated. Can you figure it out?"

"Probably, if I wasn't in this cave. I need to try different things, and I can't majick here at all."

"So let's get out of here," I told her.

"You can try that barrier if you like, but you won't get through. It's some kind of dark light that won't let any other light pass. It actually blocks your light-body."

"So what do we do?" I asked.

"Take turns sleeping, I guess, till one of us gets an idea."

It was my turn to sleep—for the third time—but hunger and thirst were getting the better of me. Sleep only came in fits. After waking again to my stomach's growl and my cobwebby mouth, I said, "You sleep, Star. I'm not tired."

She didn't answer. When I looked, I couldn't find her. The cave entrance, I discovered, was no longer blocked, and I stood on the hillside outside it shouting, "Star!" But I knew what she'd done, and I understood the fox's threat of despair.

I had no idea what to do, but thirst was harassing me awfully. I cupped my hands and had Naiadae condense me a little water. Now that I was out of that cave, my majick was once again available.

I wanted to find Star. The fox had spoken of his "demesne," but I had no idea where that might be. I started down the hillside and came to a spring that trickled downhill as a tiny, babbling brook. There was something compelling about the spring, and I stopped to drink.

The glowing light of the brook sparkled as it left the ground at its source. I drank deeply of the cool, sweet water and splashed it on my face. Suddenly I saw, or maybe *felt*, a glow in the air around the little spring. I could feel my anxiety over Star diminish. Immediately, the idea to climb high in a Zephre cocoon seemed almost to compel me.

I rose high, high into that night—high enough to see the ocean far to the east. Then I noticed the light there, like a beacon burning bright over the sea due east of me. Having no other clue, and no place else to go, I called lines and raised them to my height. Without Star to charge my hands, I'd want to do this quickly.

LVI
Parting is No Sweet Sorrow

One night, on what was becoming, "our beach," Claireth and I built a little fire and sat beside it, gently kissing and petting. "Do you hear something?" I asked her.

Perking up her precious ears, she said, "Rovers. They're here. How did I not hear them on the ether?"

We stood as a dozen Rovers fluttered down around us. "Why are you here?" Claireth asked.

"We were called," one of them told her.

"Who called?" she asked, but none of them seemed to know.

We stood looking at one another for a moment, and I think I felt her again before she arrived. When her brilliant light appeared over the ocean, peace accompanied it. I smiled and looked at Claireth, but saw her eyes full of tears. "Please don't go," she said in a voice so sad and sweet it nearly broke my heart.

Ariel walked us away from the Rovers, a hand on each of our shoulders. Then she stopped and knelt in front of us, bringing her magnificent face close to ours. "I know your bond is strong, a stronger one than I've ever seen, but I must separate you for a time." Claireth's tears sparked in the sand as she spoke. "I've brought your friends to comfort you," she said, placing her hand on my sad little darling's cheek. "Be brave till I return."

"You'll bring her back to me!" Claireth sobbed. "Please tell me you'll bring her back."

"Even Luminae can't make demands of the Universe," Ariel said. "Its jokes and tricks, its passionate plays, are mysterious to all. But this I can promise—I will bring all my light and intellect to bear on solving the problem of reuniting such devoted friends and loves. You must trust me, lovely HalfFire. That very trust may win the day."

Just then, some of the Rovers started pointing at the sky. "Look," they called. "Something falls!"

I managed to look through Zephrae eyes, but that majick was all but gone from me. Still, I could see it was Daddy falling to us on lines. He was going too fast. Suddenly, the lines he was riding looped up and tossed him fifty meters out into the sea. When he landed with a splash, the Rovers giggled nervously, and one—Ellannah, I think—said, "That looks like fun!"

Daddy swam quickly to shore, dropped to his knees in the sand, and embraced me. Through his sobs he said softly, "I've missed you so much, Kimikin. I've missed my little girl." After a bit he released me, and took Claireth into his arms. "I've missed you too," he told her. "My *other* little girl."

Finally, Daddy looked up at Ariel and said, "He has Star."

"I know," she smiled. "Your daughter and I go now to rescue her."

"Take me with you!" he said.

"Where we are going, you cannot follow. But you can help. Our little FireSprites here, your daughters, are fiercely bound. While we're away, you must use all your majick to comfort this one. Her Rovers are here to help." After whispering something in Daddy's ear, she said, "Spin down now, Kimikin."

I kissed Claireth once more, and when I drew away she choked a wretched sob. "Soon!" I told her with a smile. Then I spun down to tiny and perched on Ariel's shoulder, hiding myself under her fragrant and shining hair.

LVII
Dropping into Despair

Whatever peace had accompanied me at the spring disappeared as I fell onto those lines. Suddenly I knew, without a doubt, that I'd find my daughter down there with that beacon of light. All my thought and feeling and majick were bent to getting me there. Too much had been taken from me. I couldn't get to her quickly enough, and became like a lightless Fierae bolt striking toward the sea...

...and failed to slow myself in time. Fortunately, Father had told me about how he and Mother had overshot once in a blazing fall to the sea from a place overlooking Tara. Remembering his tale, I looped my lines and vaulted out into the water.

I could see my daughter standing with the Luminae and her little love Claireth. Many other FireSprites stood nearby on the beach. I swam with all my might. The usually friendly sea felt like a million fingers holding me back, so urgent was my need to embrace my child. When, finally, she was in my arms, emotion broke from me and I shed what tears my dehydrated body would allow. Then I hugged little Claireth to me as well. I looked up at the Luminae, and told her the fox had taken Star.

She and Kimikin would rescue her, she told me, and I could not accompany them. Somehow, though I hated it, I knew not to argue this. "You must use all your majick and love to comfort this one," she said, touching Claireth's pale gold hair. Then she came to me and whispered in my ear, "Don't let her die."

Kimikin spun herself tiny, and settled on the Luminae's shoulder. Then that brilliant being walked out over the water, flashed brighter and disappeared. The wail that came from Claireth ran up my spine, and the other FireSprites, her Rovers, gathered around and held her—stroking her hair and purring in soft little trills. At first I felt helpless, as Claireth began to shake. Then I spoke with all my effort to the Naiadae, and they condensed a shimmering mist over her. Though her eyes still seemed lost in despair, her shaking stopped, and I joined the Rovers. With my palm on her cheek, I smiled and said, "Stay with me, little daughter." For a moment I saw recognition in her eyes.

LVIII
Codicil

I couldn't tell where we were, as I was well hidden away on Ariel's shoulder. Then I heard her call, "I've come to parlay, Prince of Dawn! Will you allow me into your little universe, your little Hades?"

"My Hades serves me well, Seraph!" I heard the fox say. "Better served than endlessly serving. But come! Enter! I'm interested to hear what you could possibly have to say. Of course, you'll diminish here, and may find it unpleasant."

I felt us move, and Ariel's light dimmed. "Is this what you've come to see?" the fox said. "Yes, I have her. And there's no escape from this place."

"For all the good it will do you," I heard Mother say. "I'll do nothing for your aid or comfort."

"Oh, there are so many ways to coerce you," the fox said. "Perhaps I'll bring that body-changed brother of yours here and torment him a bit."

"You promised to leave him be!" Mother shouted.

"And I have, for the nonce," the fox told her. "But your intransigence may rub off on me. I may desire a better arrangement."

When I heard him talk about Daddy like that I became angry. But I calmed it, and came out from under Ariel's hair. The fox was now a beautiful boy—slender, and taller than a spun-up Sprite. "Why must you be so horrid?" I said in my tiny voice.

"What's this?" the boy asked. "Have you brought me another?"

"She's invited," Ariel told him. "She came with me and will leave with me. I took pity on her desire to say farewell to her mother. She is in my light, DawnPrince, and you dare not touch her."

"Tricks and subterfuge as usual, Seraph. But no matter, I have this one, though I admit, *that* one has more potential. I've seen the trails of this one's majick, but that one's trails intrigued me more. Even she doesn't know where they lead."

"Would you really rather have me?" I asked him.

"I would," he answered.

"Then I'll trade. Let my mother leave with Ariel, and I'll stay and do whatever you like, whatever I can."

"*Really?*" the boy said, his eyes wide. "Spin yourself up. Come away from that Seraph and I'll agree."

"Oh no you don't!" Mother cried, and I could see her calling up her fire.

But the boy stepped over to her and casually slapped her with the back of his hand. Mother fell as if dead, and didn't move.

"Agree!" I shouted at him.

"I do so!" he called back.

I spun myself up and walked over to him.

Ariel scooped Mother into her arms. "It seems our parlay ends," she said, and her light seemed to come back a bit, and flow into Mother.

"Yes," the boy smiled. "This is *quite* agreeable. Look what you've fetched for me! How accommodating!"

"Look closely, DawnPrince," Ariel said. "What do you have? A FireSprite to keep you company?"

The boy came over and looked at me closely. Then he scowled, and screamed, "What have you done?"

"What have *you* done?" Ariel answered. "By *your* machinations she was brought here and led down this path. I simply finished it."

"More tricks!" the boy shouted, his face red and contorted. "But I'll have that one again, rest assured!" he said, indicating my mother, cradled in Ariel's arms.

"To what purpose?" Ariel smiled. "Look closely at this one as well. What do you see?"

"You've changed her, too?" the boy cried out. "This is meddling beyond your license! You've created, and you've destroyed! These were the only aneke'lementals, and you've ruined them!"

"Again," Ariel smiled, "all begun by your machinations."

"It's tenuous and flimsy, Ariel Seraph! RealmWhite will censure you for this!"

"RealmWhite sanctioned this course," she told him.

"No! How! It's meddlesome in the extreme!"

"Nonetheless," Ariel smiled.

"Fine!" he shouted, red with rage. "I'll keep this one for spite, and torment her endlessly. Take that thought with you as you leave."

164

"Here's a thought for you," Ariel said. "The terms of your internment here, the terms of the thousand years, specify that you kill no HalfFire: Fairae, Dakini or Sprite. This one is LoveLocked to another, who is even now dying without her. If she dies, it will be by your action, and the thousand years will begin again. It was well worded, little Prince, that you and your Third must endure a thousand years in BorderRealm without causing the death of a single HalfFire. With so few of the thousand years left, are you willing to reset the count?" Ariel was no longer smiling. She glared down at the boy, and her expression was fierce. "What say you, Morning Star?"

"Take her," he said, his voice a low growl. "Soon I'll have men to tempt again."

"Come quickly!" Ariel said to me. "Back on my shoulder, little one! I fear for Claireth!"

"If she dies now, it's no fault of mine!" the boy said. "You brought her here, and she leaves as she came."

"Yes," Ariel agreed, and in a moment we were walking over the sea.

LIX
Love Torn

I understood loss and grief and sorrow, but the love bond between my daughter and Claireth was something well beyond my human understanding. The Rovers purred and trilled to her, and at one point the sound seemed to become a wail. All my majick I bent to comforting that child, and in the end my majick failed. I could feel her slipping away.

Finally I stood and faced the sea. "You must come back *now!*" I screamed, and a tremendous light blazed in the tears filling my eyes.

LX
Love Torn

I flew from Ariel's shoulder, and spun up on the beach. Daddy was standing with tears streaming down his cheeks. When I saw her in the Rovers' arms, I wailed a sound I could not have made as a human. Her glow was gone. Other than Daddy, she was the only thing without that light.

That wailing cry I'd sounded drained me completely, and I fell to my knees. My claws grew, and I raked them down my cheeks. Then I looked up and saw Ariel. I had never seen her sad, and it was more than I could bear. I wailed again, was about to push my claws through my throat when Ariel said, "No," and my claws disappeared. Then I saw it.

A tear, like a star falling from her eye, rolled down her cheek. Smiling, she placed her palms on my face and I could feel the tearing I'd done mend. Then she walked to where the Rovers had Claireth—all of them sparking tears in the sand—and said, again, "No!"

Ariel took that star tear from her cheek and balanced it on her finger. Then she touched it to Claireth's forehead. I watched as the light of it spread over my darling, and my own tears came again, this time for joy.

She opened her eyes looking directly at me, and smiled. Then, to Ariel, she said in a weak voice, "You kept your promise."

Ariel exhaled a tremendous sigh, smiled and said, "For *this*, I will be censured."

"No you won't," Daddy told her. "Love is above the rules."

Between the fox-boy's slap and Ariel's majick, Mother slept through pretty much everything. When she awoke, Ariel took her and me aside. She wanted to talk to us before she departed. To Mother, she said, "Do you understand what has happened?"

"The fox doesn't have us anymore," Mother said, "so I'm guessing what happened was good."

"Call to the Naiadae," Ariel told her.

Mother's brow furrowed, and she said in a worried voice, "I can barely hear them, barely *feel* them."

"I once said it might be better if you two aneke'lementals went to the Fierae," Ariel told her.

"But you said you wouldn't force such a thing."

"Circumstances and the Universe's pranks walked you down this road. I did what I had to in order to save you both. You're a FireSprite now, Star FieraeBorn."

Mother plopped down on her arse, and I thought she would cry. "All the Fierae went through to plot that trace, to bring about aneke'lementals. Finished! Ended! Gone from World!"

"How do you know what traces the Fierae were plotting?" Ariel asked. "Perhaps they wanted to build a bridge between two worlds. Both of you still have the crossing majick, and any you bear, however born, will have it. For all I know, you may even be able to teach it. You are, after all, amazing creatures...or at least you were. Now you're amazing HalfFire."

The Rovers lifted Claireth and fluttered gently skyward. They would take her to ClanHome, and I would go with them. "I can't leave her alone," I told Mother and Daddy. "Meet us in ClanHome."

"How do we get there?" Daddy asked.

"I *know*!" Mother told him, her eyes wide. "I know where it is."

LXI
ClanHome

"I can ride lines west to the forest, but I'll have to hike the rest of the way. We should have gotten one of the Rovers to spin me down. You could have flown me there on your shoulder," I laughed.

The instant I said it, I was spun tiny, and Star gently scooped me up into her hands. Holding me up to her shoulder, she said, "Climb on!"

"How did you do that?" I asked her. "Where did you get that kind of majick?"

"I'll explain it to you later," she said. "Now hold onto my hair, and don't fall off. It might be jarring if I have to swoop down and catch you."

"Fly carefully!" I implored. "I'm still recovering from being a ghost!"

We both walked into ClanHome tiny. Once I was off her shoulder, and my stomach settled, I started pestering her about that majick. How had she learned to spin? "Right now," she told me, "it's a secret. But I'll tell you soon."

"How many times, Star, have you said to me, 'No secrets!'?"

"A few," she said. "But I'll keep this one for now to protect you. Please don't ask me again. I hate saying no to you."

"But you *are* going to tell me?" I persisted.

"Yes," she answered. "Or you'll learn. Now let's find Kimikin and Claireth."

"I take it you're okay with those two now?" I said.

"Cute as cuddlebugs," Star smiled, "And soon to be fat as grapes!"

"And you don't want to make Kimi human again?"

"I couldn't if I did, but I don't."

"You don't want to take her home?"

"She *is* home, Spearl."

Because she was pregnant, the Rovers brought Claireth to BornHome, which was on the northern outskirts of ClanHome. The surgeons examined her and told us, "She's LoveLocked."

"I *know* she's LoveLocked," Star said.

"I seriously know it," I added.

"As bad as it must have been for her," the surgeon said, "I'm surprised she didn't tear herself. She needs to rest, *with her locked lover beside her!* For *days!* How in helluva did they get separated?"

"My daughter came to rescue me," Star said.

"And Claireth didn't join her in that quest?"

"It was dangerous," Star told him.

"So is LoveLock! Never take it lightly," he said sternly. "Thank the Inward Light it doesn't happen that often!"

LXII
BornHome

We flew through night with Claireth borne by six Rovers. They flew her straight to BornHome, where we found that her babe was fine. But she needed rest. Lots of rest with me cuddlebugged to her side. The BornHome Sprites brought us berries to eat, and even a little mead. It was such a relief to feel safe. It was such a relief to be together again.

After several nights cuddly rest, Claireth was well again, and we decided to leave BornHome. But the Sprites there told us we should stay. "You're both about to begin swelling, we can already see it. Once that starts, it won't be long."

"Sounds like it may happen faster here than in that other world," I told Claireth.

"Once they swell, it goes fast. Especially if we eat the right things."

"Will they make us lie abed if we stay here?" I asked.

"Not till we want to. We can wander BornHome and play with babes, or go out to ClanHome if we like. But they'll want us to stay close, and to check in pretty often. And if we want," she whispered, "we can come back, climb into bed, and they'll bring us berries and honeyed water. It's nice to be brought things while lying about, don't you think?"

"Yes," I told her. "Though I wonder if it's nice for those bringing."

"The BornHome Sprites wouldn't do this if they didn't want to. It's fun for them, and they have lots of babes to play with."

While Claireth was recovering, Mother and Daddy came several times to see us. I could tell by the way Mother looked at me that she hadn't told him yet. I wasn't sure why, but started to understand later when Claireth and I went to meet them in a little ClanHome park. We saw Daddy first, sitting alone with a mug of mead. We were about to run to him, when we saw, not far away, Mother and Roth flutter down from the clouds. "If I didn't know better, and of course I don't, I'd say those two have a LoveLink," Claireth said to me.

"That might be hard on Daddy," I said.

"Your father is a *wonderful* creature," Claireth huffed. "How dare you call him jealous!"

"I didn't say jealous," I told her.

"Oh!" she chirped. "I guess you didn't."

Mother and Roth were walking toward Daddy. "Let's go see them," I said.

Daddy seemed a bit in his cups, and at some point I said to him, "Why don't you get some wings?"

Mother showed me a little scowl, as if she didn't want me suggesting that. Why? "Maybe I will," Daddy said in a tipsy tone. For some reason, I made a scowling face at Mother.

"Claireth," Mother said. "Go sit on Spearl's lap. He's missed you."

Without a thought, Claireth plopped down on Daddy, and said, "I missed you, too. I wish I could call you Daddy. It's such a cutie pie sound when Kimikin says it."

"I told you once before you're my daughter now," he said. "And I *insist* that you call me Daddy."

"And I'll be your little HalfFire girl," she said.

While Claireth and Daddy had one another's attentions, Mother pulled me aside. "Don't get him thinking about wings," she told me.

"Why not?" I said, hands on my hips. "Does it have something to do with Roth?"

Mother didn't say anything for a moment, as if she was conflicted. Finally she said, "The Luminae warned me against it. She said he'd never be happy as a Sprite."

"Well, he's not going to be happy here without wings, and with you Fluttering off with Roth. I know he wouldn't be jealous, but he'll miss you. There will come a time when you won't want to love him because he's not HalfFire; I can see it in your nature. You already know that, don't you?"

"Yes, Kimikin, I know. I have a plan for him, but not yet. I want him to see his grandbabies born, first."

"What is your plan, Mother?" I asked, and she told me.

Claireth and I had started sleeping, something FireSprites rarely do unless they're hurt, or ill, or have buns in their ovens. One night, we woke up in our BornHome bed face to face. "Claireth," I said.

"Mmmm," she said, still waking. "What is it, Cutie Pie?"

"Our bellies are touching."

Claireth pulled the silky little coverlet off us. Looking down she said, "They've jumped out a bit!" Then a BornHome Sprite came over and said, "You two should stay here, now. When they jump like that, there's no telling when the screaming will start."

"I'll be screaming?" I said, eyes wide.

"Don't worry, we'll help," she smiled. "But you should know what's coming, and it's our job to tell you. It's the accepted thought on the subject."

"I think she's saying yes," Claireth frowned.

LXIII
Human Feelings

Star and Roth became lovers. At first, perhaps, she tried not to be obvious about it, but that no longer seemed to concern her. I was not jealous, but I was hurt that she no longer cared for my touch. One night, she came to me in the park at ClanHome and said, "Look, Spearl, over there looking at you. Isn't that the Fairae girl Lila? Go to her. She wants you to play again."

Without saying a word, I got up and went over to Lila. "Hello," she said. "Would you like to play? It's so different with you, I'd like to try it again."

"Will you talk to me for a while first?" I asked.

"Oh yes!" she squeaked. "Talking is the bestest foreplay!"

For some reason, I told Lila about Star and Roth, and how Star no longer seemed to want me. "It happens," she said. "LoveLinks don't last, unless they become LoveLocks, of course, but that's rare. You aren't jealous, are you?" she asked, obviously a little upset by the idea.

"No. Just a bit hurt." I told her.

"We're allowed to hurt when a love moves on. We are half creature, after all, and you are nearly *all*. Come with me and let me love away some of your hurt. I won't get it all, but time will take the rest." Then she looked over to where Star and Roth were sitting and said, "Tell me, what is it about her that links you so?"

"She's human," I told her.

Lila looked again, and said, "She's a FireSprite. Humans don't glow."

"I think she had the surgeons do that because Roth likes it," I said.

"No," Lila told me. "She's a FireSprite."

Though my heart wasn't in it, I'd promised myself to Lila, and her inquisitive love turned out to be pleasant. But my little bit of hurt festered, as I remembered Star saying, after promising to eventually tell me her secret, "Or you'll learn."

Once my dear sister, mate and mother of my child in a second life, and now someone, some*thing*, I couldn't understand. LoveLinks and LoveLocks were beyond my comprehension, but I knew I loved Star. I'd been forced to love her twice, in two different ways. The sister I'd loved was taken away. Now it seemed I'd lose her as my life-mate as well.

I remembered that time at Smith's Crossing when I decided to take Kimmy home with me. Star had become so angry, and then she'd cried, heartbroken that I'd found someone "human"—someone *like me*. I could only wonder if the Universe smiled or frowned at such ironies.

For a while, I thought about going to the surgeons. But I simply could not. I missed my world, missed human people and the New Apprentices who looked to me for advice and wisdom. They all had visions of what World could be, and though they sometimes differed, they were all beautiful and inspired by love. *Human* love. No, if Star really was a FireSprite, irretrievable to humanity, I would leave her to this love I couldn't understand. I'd find a way back to my world, slip away and be gone. My heartbreak lied to me and said she wouldn't even miss me. Despair crept in and told me the lie was true. I wandered off looking for Lila. I needed a favor.

LXIV
A Little Fey, a Little Baby

"I want my pack!" I said to Claireth as we woke to our bellies one night in BornHome.

"Your what?" she asked, giggling.

"Remember when you got me down out of that tree? We left my pack hanging there, and I want it."

"I seem to recall rescuing a little *human* girl once who was trapped in such a garment. But you *can't* be her. You're too cute!" she said, smothering me with kisses.

Though not right away, I said, "Stop kissing!" Then I showed her an awful pout. "I want my pack," I said in a petulant cutie pie whine.

Claireth rolled on her back, put her hands behind her head and said, "Then we'll find it. As soon as the babes come, and can fly, or at least hang on, we'll go."

I rolled over on top of her, which was a precarious thing considering our bellies, and said, "I want my pack *now*." Then I pecked her a kiss.

"What has made you think of it after all this time? You know," she told me, "we often get a little fey just before it happens, and this sounds like fey talk to me. Why do you want that silly thing? You wouldn't *wear* it where people could see?" she said with a little pout of her own.

"There are things in it that I want," I told her. "There's a treasure in there I'll give to you if you'll help me find it. And a little book Daddy gave me that I haven't finished writing."

"What kind of treasure?" she asked me, her eyebrows lifting.

I snuggled down close to her, and whispered in her ear, "A *mirror!*"

"No!" she said, holding me away by the shoulders.

"Yes," I smiled.

Conspiring now, Claireth said, "I know almost exactly where I found you, and it's not *too* far. If we hurry, they won't even miss us. But if they see us leaving, we'll tell them we've urgent Rover business, and will be right back. I've heard tales of mirrors, and the majick they can do. They say some witches keep them, and tell themselves how beautiful they are."

"It's true," I told her. "Remember, I was a witch in the other world, and my mirror thought I was very pretty."

"I do, too!" she said, instigating more play.

But I stopped us and said, "No time. Let's go before these bellies pop and our babes keep us here and busy."

"Okay," she agreed. "Just act normal and we'll walk right out."

I wasn't sure what Claireth meant about being a little fey near the end, but I was feeling wonderful. We were two plump, ripe FireSprites out in the world again. "ClanHome is nice," I said to Claireth as we fluttered around looking for that tree. "But I like being out here. I miss being a Rover."

"Why? Did you quit?" Claireth asked, a shocked look on her face.

"No!" I told her. "But I miss *patrolling!*"

"Oh!" she chirped. "That's different."

"I'll always be your little Fourth!" I told her, flying up to kiss her cheek.

"Third," she told me. "I heard it on the ether. Some wanted to make you *Second!*"

"I have to be Third, first," I told her. "I want no special treatment because my lover is the fearsome First Claireth!"

"*No* special treatment?" she asked with that look in her eye.

"Well," I blushed. "You're always welcome to treat me that kind of special."

When we found my pack, I spun up and retrieved it. "Are you ready for your treasure?" I asked Claireth.

"Oh, I so want to see a mirror!" she cooed. "But it will be *ours.* Now take it out and let's look at our bellies in it."

Claireth was enthralled by that little mirror, and I was happy to have my book back. I might not be an Apprentice anymore, I thought, but I'll at least finish the book Daddy gave me.

Still big, we were taking turns holding the mirror for each other to look at our rounding tummies. Claireth was holding it for

177

me, and giggling terribly, when I felt a shocking pain, and saw my belly jump out. Suddenly, it looked like a melon.

Claireth stopped giggling and said, "Uh oh!"

After another pain, worse than before, I said, "Quick, let's spin down and fly back to BornHome!" Then another pain knocked me onto my arse. "Ooowww!" I yowled.

"Don't you dare spin down!" Claireth told me. "Your babe comes! If you're tiny and helpless, a bird might swoop down and eat you!"

"Wouldn't you protect me?" I cried, the pain becoming pretty much unbelievable.

"I can't protect and pull a babe out of you at the same time! A bird would eat us both!"

"You mean it's going to happen *here*?" I moaned.

"Sooner or later," she said. "But you're definitely not going anywhere till it's done!"

"Ooowww!" I howled.

"Be brave, Rover Third!" Claireth told me. Then she giggled and said, "I wonder what it will be!"

It seemed like a very long time, and an awfully lot of pain, before Claireth said, "I can see it coming, head first! I've heard that makes it easier."

"I should hope so!" I screamed. My body seemed about to split in two.

"Shall I hold the mirror so you can watch it come?" Claireth asked.

"No! Silly bitch!" I shouted. "Get it out, out, out!"

Then I heard a little wail, and the pain miraculously ceased. "A boy babe!" Claireth cried, holding him high over her head. "What will you call him?"

"You give him a name," I said. "I'm too tired."

"Oh thank you!" she said. "And you shall name mine!"

"They're *ours*!" I told her.

"Yes," she said, kneeling down to kiss me. "Now take our babe and see if he'll feed. The sooner the bet...OOOWWW!"

"Oh no!" I said, watching Claireth's belly pop out to ripe-size. "Why couldn't you have gone first? I'm exhausted!"

Flopping onto her back, Claireth yowled, "Get it out! *Please*, Cutie Pie! Get it out of me, you little bitch!"

Giggling, holding a feeding babe to my breast, I sprinkled a little of my dust on her nose and said, "Push!"

LXV
Enormous and Clothed

By the time I found Lila, I think her desire to experiment with human love had waned. I almost felt guilty that I'd never really been in the mood. I could have tried harder for her. But I could also tell that she still considered me a friend—perhaps even dear. "Could you do something for me, Lila?" I asked.

"It isn't play you want, is it? I don't see it in your eyes."

"No. I was wondering if you could spin me up to my normal size."

"What *is* your normal size?" she asked.

"About six feet."

"*Six feet!*" she howled. "That's enormous! I'm not a FireSprite, you know, and may not be strong enough for all those feet!"

"It's okay, Lila," I said, my sadness obviously showing.

With a look of compassion, she said, "Come with me. I know of a brook nearby. My majick is always a little stronger near running water."

At Kimikin's request, some north-patrolling Rovers had located and retrieved my pack. Star had left it by that tree when she went off with the fox in his guise as the human child "Shine." Gryn was still in its sheath. It was the first time I realized that it didn't follow me around in this world, nor did it glow. I believe, in BorderRealm, it was basically a big knife.

I'd carried my pack when I went to find Lila, intending to dress and put it on so my meager possessions would be spun up with me. When I opened it, I saw Star's clothes in there as well. I held them up, then saw Lila looking at me. "I'm not that kind of girl," she blushed.

Lila was a bit embarrassed to have me dressed in her presence, but said, "I try to keep an open mind. Still, I'm glad we're out here where nobody can see us."

With all her little might, she spun me up to something like my normal height. She stayed tiny, as it took all her majick to

180

achieve this feat. "Good-bye, Spearl," she said, buzzing up to my ear. "I hope you find your world, and that they don't run screaming when they see you coming in those clothes."

She was about to fly off when I said, "Wait!" Star's clothes were still lying tiny on the ground. I tore off a little corner of my shirttail and tied them into it. "Give these to Star for me," I told Lila. "Tell her I've gone home."

LXVI
Walking Big to BornHome

Claireth named our son Elloreth, and I named the girl she bore Pearl. "I know it's not a FireSprite name," I told her. "But it was my grandmother's, and she was a great human witch. Our mirror belonged to her."

"It's a lovely name," Claireth said.

"Not a cutie pie name?" I asked.

"Not every cutie pie gets a cutie pie name," she smiled.

Our babes were identical in all ways but one. Had they not been different genders, we'd never have been able to tell them apart. "I'm ready to go back to BornHome and let them bring us things," I told Claireth.

"We might as well walk back," she told me.

"Why would we walk?" I asked her.

"Feel your light," she told me.

"Oh!" I said. "I can't spin!"

"Not for a day or two," she said.

"I can still fly, though," I told her.

"And what will you do if we fly to BornHome, plop down on it and squish it with your arse?"

We both giggled at that thought, then I said, "It's a lovely summon for a walk, anyway."

With soft, sweet grasses, Claireth and I lined my pack and snuggled our babes inside. Then we each took a strap and swung them between us as we walked. FireSprite Babes are more aware at birth than human ones. Pearl and Elloreth smiled and squeaked little giggles as they rode between their two mamas.

Along the way back to BornHome, Claireth and I stopped to pick blackberries. We were both a bit hungry. "If we could just spin down we could fill up on one or two of these," I said.

"I *know!*" Claireth agreed. "It's fun to be big and eat big things like fish, but this is such a waste of berries!"

"You know," I told her. "There's a fat hare in those bushes behind us. You just keep picking berries, and I'll saunter around behind him."

"Don't scare him off," she said in a harsh whisper. "I'm hungry, and hares are yummy when you're hungry."

Spun down, FireSprites are *very* fast. But even big Sprites are quicker than any human could ever be—or any hare. In a minute, I came back to Claireth with the hare bleeding out where I'd opened his throat with my foreclaw. I held it up for her to see, and smiled. "Oh!" she chirped. "You're just so cute when your fangs come out!"

While our hare roasted on a hickory switch, Claireth and I each grabbed a babe and fed them. She'd gotten Elloreth, and said, "I'm taking Pearl next time. This tiny Rover suckles me sore!"

"If you think Pearl's so much better, I'll swap with you now," I told her.

"Yes!" she said.

Not a minute after we swapped, she said, "You're right! She's worse!"

The babes were asleep in my pack, and Claireth and I were lounging, patting our hare-stuffed bellies. With a little burp, she said, "I'm full. But not so full as I was before Pearl popped out!"

"Do you hear something?" I asked her.

"I was wondering when you'd notice, Rover Third," Claireth smiled. "Rovers are coming. How many do you hear?"

"Four," I told her. "Ellannah, Stuben, Roth and...wait...the fourth isn't a Rover. It's my mother."

"Really?" Claireth said, her eyes wide. "I thought for sure it was four Rovers. Maybe we *should* have made you a Second!"

As the Rovers plus one fluttered in, they spun big and dropped down around us. Mother squinted her eyes at me. "Where have you two been? They're worried sick at BornHome and..." Then she saw Elloreth and Pearl sleeping in my pack. "Oh, they're such cutie pies!" she cooed.

But her change in tone didn't mollify me. I marched over to her and said, with squinty eyes of my own, "Don't you ever talk to me like that again! I'm a Rover Second, and you'll show a little respect!"

"Rover Third," Claireth said.

"Second!" I told her through a scowl.

"That's what I meant!" she demurred.

"Yes! Second!" the other Rovers agreed.

"I'm sorry," Mother said, quite contritely. "I was just a little worried. Can I hold them, please?"

Mother sparked a few tears on the ground when I told her Pearl's name, and said "Elloreth" was also lovely. After she'd shared our babes with the Rovers, who wanted to cuddle them as well, she held up a small cloth tied up like a sack. "Spearl sent these to me with Lila." Then she whispered, "They're my clothes."

"Where is he?" I asked.

"She said he's spun up enormous and dressed. He told her he's going home."

"He *can't* go home!" I told her. "One of us would have to take him. Couldn't you have paid him a little attention? What's *wrong* with you?" I chided.

At that moment, I was so angry I just wanted to take a switch to her. But when she plopped down on her arse and started crying, I wasn't sure what to do. She was acting very un-motherlike. Then Claireth sidled up to me and said, "Be gentle with her. When the Luminae Lady touched her light to you, she made you change slowly, over time, till you were finally my cutie pie Sprite. But to save you both, she had to change Star all at once. It was a shock. She became what she is hard and fast. She's a FireSprite true. Though she can remember being 'Mother' and Daddy's mate, she can't feel it anymore. I suspect even her memory will fade a bit with time." Then she sat beside Mother and took her in her arms. "It's okay, Star," she said. "Kimikin isn't angry with you."

"StarShine," Mother said through her sniffles. "I'm StarShine."

Five Rovers and a pretty HalfFire called StarShine walked toward BornHome, taking turns carrying babes, and suckling them from time to time. With Elloreth in her arms, Mother walked beside me and said, "I have to take him home, Kimikin. Somewhere, deep inside, it saddens me that I hurt Spearl so. I'll go search for him now, and won't stop till he's found and I've taken him home."

184

She started to hand Elloreth to me, but I said, "Wait, Mother."

"StarShine," she said softly.

I went to Ellannah, who had Pearl at that moment, and asked if she and the other Rovers would go find Daddy. "He's enormous and clothed. You should spot him pretty easily. Take Mother...take StarShine with you."

Ellannah smiled, and whispered, "I know you're Second now, but so am I. I need a First to tell me if it's to be an order."

"It's a request," I told her.

"Oh!" she chirped. "That's different."

StarShine and the Rovers flew off to find Daddy. We were about to put the babes back into my pack, when Claireth said, "I think I can spin again!"

"Me, too!" I cried. "It must have been that lovely white hare we ate!"

When I put on my pack so it would spin down with me, Claireth blushed and said, "I'm glad my Rovers are gone, you scandalous thing!"

"Tonight," I told her, "in our bed at BornHome, I'll tie a ribbon round my thigh for you."

"Oh, you're bad!" she grinned.

After being served raspberries in bed, and sips of elderberry, a BornHome Sprite called Naneth put Pearl and Elloreth in a cradle beside us. "They need to get used to sleeping without you," she told us with authority. "And you two need *rest*. You should love a little, then sleep!" Noticing the ribbon lying on the bed next to me, Naneth blushed. "A *little* love," she giggled as she left.

"They're very open-minded here," Claireth whispered to me.

LXVII
A Real Bastard

I had my bearings, and was headed, walking, toward where my home would be if I was...well, if I was *home*. I'd made it to what would be the Ninety-five, and was heading south. I had sorrow and despair keeping me company, and occasionally caught myself leaking tears. Finally I stopped, weary with sadness, and sat against a little tree. "Your home won't be there, of course," I heard him say.

"What do you want?" I asked.

"Just to talk," he said. "Oh, I could probably get away with killing you, but who knows. Some humans are damn near HalfFire. You just can't seem to realize it. Anyway, it would serve no purpose. I doubt it would bother Star. Actually, they call her StarShine now. StarShine HalfFire. She's got a little LoveLink going on with a Rover, but I think you know that."

"You really are a bastard," I laughed, tears still in my eyes.

"Literally," he told me. "Would you like to go home? Want me to take you back to your world?" he purred.

"I want nothing by your auspices," I told him.

"Well, that's a little harsh," the fox said. "What did I ever do to you?"

"Very funny," I muttered.

"It's good to keep a sense of humor. But I really will take you home if you like, no strings attached...well, okay, maybe a *thread* or two."

"Fug off," I said.

"The word was actually 'fuck'," he told me, "before humans became an endangered species and forgot half their words. Fuck, fuck, fuck! A very versatile expletive."

"So *fuck* off," I amended.

"As you please," he said. "Won't be long now and I'll be back on the good old Earth, anyway, teaching men to be men and women how to get what they want from them. It'll be such fun! Maybe I'll see you there, if you find a way home. I wouldn't wager on it, though. I suspect that majick died when Seraph Bitchboy did away with aneke'lementals."

"She changed Star?" I asked.

"You didn't know that?" he said. "Oh, she's meddlesome. They all are. Claim harmony with the Universe's will, then jump in and diddle the sauce. Hypocrites of the first order!"

For a moment, I felt anger at what he'd told me about Star and the Luminae. But it calmed immediately, and I said, "Her love is wise, and I think unassailable. Whatever her reasons, I accept them. The Luminae are incredible beings."

"*I'm* a Luminae," he told me, though he almost sounded perturbed by it.

"You're a deceiver," I said. "Why don't you leave me alone."

"I will," the fox said. "Very alone. You're the only living boy in New York."

"What?" I snorted

"From a very old song," he told me. "It means you're on your own, kiddo. Maybe you should take that short sword of yours and open up an artery. Femoral's good, on the inside of your thigh."

"Please go away," I said.

"Well, since you used the majick word," he chuckled as he disappeared.

The fox's suggestion to put Gryn to use kept echoing in my head, and for a moment it seemed a comforting thought. But I willed it away, and said to myself, "I'm an Apprentice. My life is not mine to end." Then I heard the thrumming of dragonfly wings, and four Sprites spun up around me. One of them was Star.

LXVIII
Changing Hearts

After giggly shenanigans with my love-toy ribbon, and more subtle love after, Claireth and I snuggled in our bed at BornHome. "Is StarShine really going to take Daddy back to the other world?" she asked me. "Won't you miss him? Don't you want to say good-bye? I miss him a little already just thinking about it. He comforted me so when we were parted. I wanted to tear myself, but he sprinkled me with mist, and my claws didn't come."

"I'll miss him, but StarShine must see him home alone," I told her. "She has much to say, and she has a plan that might help him. Anyway, we can go see him whenever we like. I still have the crossing majick, you know. We can take our babes to meet him."

"Oh! But they'll burn!" she cried.

"At *night*, silly Rover! We'll go only at night. I wouldn't want to have to rub aloe on your bottom again."

"Why not?" she pouted. "Don't you like my bottom?"

"I like it very much," I smiled. "Bring it here and I'll rub it right now."

The exhaustion of bearing our babes in the woods, and our day of walking, caught up with Claireth and me, and we slept quite a bit, for FireSprites. Naneth clucked at us, insisting we stay abed for at least three summons, and I think some of our sleeping was due to the elderberry she made us drink. "Running off and having babes in the wood!" she said one night as she made us sip. "Like little field mice! What if a bird had eaten you?"

"We were big!" I said, catching my breath from the elderberry.

"Oh my!" she said. "The pain must have been terrible!"

"And I had to catch Pearl after bearing Elloreth," I told her. "Can you imagine *that*?"

"No!" she said. "My poor little Rover! You rest now. I'll feed these babes myself." Then she whispered, "No playing with ribbons. Sleep!"

One night we found ourselves all slept out, and ready to be free of Naneth's attentions for a while. Gathering up Pearl and Elloreth, we snuck out and went to the park in ClanHome. While we were sitting in a patch of cool moss, I heard, "Psssst!"

I looked over to a big oak, and saw Prissi and Teali peeking around it. Claireth saw them, too, and said, "I can't believe those two would show their tails around here!"

"They look scared, sweetie," I said, touching her cheek. "Let's go see what they want."

With babes in our arms, we walked over to where the Fairae were hiding. "What?" Claireth demanded.

"*Please*, Claireth," Prissi pleaded. "Remove your mark. We're so sorry. We were tricked by that one, *honest*! We feel so terrible about it, and we're so alone!"

Both of them looked so pitiful, standing there sparking tears on the ground, that I thought Claireth would soften, but she didn't. "You should have thought of that before!" she scolded, wagging a finger at them, which made me smile.

"They really seem sorry," I said in a soft voice, hoping to calm my darling Rover. "Maybe we should forgive them. Perhaps the Universe let them be bad for a while so some good could come of it."

"What good?" Claireth asked, her brow furrowed.

"Well," I told her. "We'd never have found Ilsa so she could go to RealmWhite, and you got your bottom rubbed with aloe."

"That was nice," she smiled. Then she whispered to me, "But even if I forgive them, I can't remove their tails. It took the very limits of my majick to put them on!"

Handing Pearl into Claireth's other arm, I said, "Come here, you two, and turn around." When they had their backs to me I said, "Bend over."

With a hand on each of their tails, I closed my eyes and forgave them for true. Then I called up my majick and the marks disappeared. Giving them each a good swat on their now tailless bottoms, I said, "Now you're forgiven!"

"But if you ever..." Claireth began.

I shushed her with my fingers on her lips, and said, "*Forgiven!* Right?"

"Yes," she smiled. "You're forgiven." Then she whispered to me, "How did you *do* that?"

"I think I'm a very strong FireSprite," I told her.

"Oooooh!" she cooed. "Think how strong our babes will be!"

Before long, the four of us were sitting together cooing and purring with Pearl and Elloreth.

LXIV
Final Journey

One of the FireSprites, I think her name was Ellannah, said to Star, "We're going back to play with the babes before we have to start patrolling again."

"Thank you for helping me find him," she said.

"And *you*," Ellannah said to me, "should be ashamed of yourself, going around all enormous and clothed! We Rovers are open-minded, but *really*!"

Then they all buzzed off and I was alone with Star. I snorted a little laugh and said, "Do my clothes bother *you*?"

For answer, Star spun herself up to what used to be her normal size. Then she untied the little sack she carried, folded her wings back, and got dressed. "I *do* feel a bit naughty," she told me.

At the exact same moment that a tear slid down my cheek, one dropped from her eye and sparked on the ground. "You're very pretty," I managed to say, stifling my tears.

"Call up lines, Spearl, I can't do it anymore. We'll ride when we can and hike when we must."

"Where are we going?" I asked.

"I promised to tell you everything, and when we get where we're going, I will. Until then, let's just talk like we used to when we were brother and sister. We can be that now, you know."

I wanted to take her in my arms. I wanted to love her like we had *after* we were brother and sister. But I couldn't, I knew. I called up lines. We rode and walked for several days, camping like we used to, scooting a rabbit and a peahen out of their flesh, laughing at each other's little jokes and reminiscences. Eventually, I saw the foothills and realized where we were. "Wanda May's village would be right over there," I said, pointing.

"Yes," she smiled. "We're here. I came to visit Wanda a few nights ago. She was quite startled, at first—you know how superstitious she is—but she finally understood."

"Must have been one helluva tale for her to hear," I said.

"Helluva tale to tell," Star giggled—a sound she hadn't made in so long I'd forgotten it. "Now there are things I must tell you.

Ariel changed me in order to save Kimikin from something very horrible. It was the only way. He'd have never stopped trying to catch me if I'd stayed aneke'lemental, and would have tormented Kimikin to make me comply. Now the aneke'lementals are no more."

"Does that hurt you?" I asked.

"No," she said. "I'm HalfFire now, more so even than Kimikin. There's still an untapped well of majick in her. Either the fox can't see it, or it's not aneke'lemental. Maybe it's Luminae majick. As a Sprite, I'm kind of in awe of her. She's a Rover Second already, you know. Claireth will be so proud when she becomes First, though I think she'll miss being able to give orders."

"I miss her. I miss both of them."

"And you didn't even see your grandchildren. I was waiting on their arrival before I brought you here, but I wasn't paying attention to you, and you got away. I'm so sorry, Spearl. I thought Lila would be enough company until the twins arrived. I should have known better."

"Twins!" I said.

"Did I say twins?" she asked, seeming confused. "Well, who knows! Maybe they are—twin Sprites of different mothers! They look identical, except Elloreth is a boy and Pearl is a girl."

"Pearl!"

"Yes. Kimikin named her after our mother."

"I want to go back and see them!" I said.

"No need," she told me. "We'll bring them to you in a couple of nights. We'll come for a visit. Now let me finish telling you everything you wanted to know."

Star had a wicked gleam in her eye, and I knew she was about to surprise me with something. "What?" I asked.

"You've always wondered, and don't deny it, why I never brought Wanda May into our bed—why I kept her to myself. It's because she has a very big crush on you, and is so much *like* you, that I was afraid she'd take you away from me. And I touched your thought enough back then to know she climbed into your fantasies every once in a while."

"I..." I began, but Star put her fingers on my lips.

"Shush," she said. "Now give me a hug, and don't you dare be bashful once you're home. You've taken care of me for so long,

Spearl, through two lives. It was a burden, and don't say it wasn't. You deserve a little rest." I embraced Star, and could feel the change. We were back in our...back in *my* World.

We walked into the village, and Star tapped on Wanda May's door. The gentle flicker of oil lamps shone through the windows. When she came to let us in, Wanda May smiled at Star, and blushed when she saw me. "You know," Star said, "I need to go arrange a visit from Spearl's grandbabies. He needs some rest, Wanda May. Can I leave him with you for a while?"

Wanda's blush seemed to glow in the lamplight. "Would you like some wine?" she asked me.

"Get him some Corn!" Star said as she left. "Makes him randy!"

Wanda May's blush very nearly ignited.

LXV
Twice a Gift

The last time we went to see Daddy, Pearl and Elloreth had just turned three. Wanda May had recently given Daddy a daughter (a new sister!), and the three of them seemed very happy.

Our babes were flying and talking this visit, and had fluttered down onto Daddy's knees to hear tales. "You should put something on them," Wanda May said. "They'll catch cold."

"What does she mean?" Claireth said, her eyes squinted.

"Hush," I told her. Then to Wanda May I said, "None of that, now. Remember what I told you."

"What did you tell her?" Claireth wanted to know.

"That FireSprites don't catch cold."

Not long after that visit, I finished the book Daddy gave me with what I am writing now. Tomorrow night, I'll sneak in and leave it for him. Maybe he'll read it to his grandbabies some day, and to his little daughter Lila.

LXVI
Joining

I found Kimikin's journal beside me on my pillow one morning, not long after she'd visited with Pearl and Elloreth. It was as big a surprise as I'm sure she'd intended. She must be very stealthy, as Wanda and I are both light sleepers. Especially with a baby in the house.

Once I'd finished reading her journal—her incredible tale—I decided to go a ways from the village and talk with the Fierae. It had been a long time, and I had questions. Of course, having questions for the Fierae doesn't mean you'll get answers. Still, I wanted to try.

I'd already called up a little storm party just to the east of us. As I was walking out the door, Wanda May stopped me. "Take a drink of this before you go," she said, handing me the molasses tonic. "I'm cooking pig's liver tonight, so hurry home." Then her eyes misted and she whispered, "Please be careful."

"How do you always know what I'm going to do before I do it?" I asked her with a smile.

"I promised Star I'd take care of you," she said.

"StarShine," I told her.

I found a ground charge in a tall pine, chittering to beat all helluva. "She comes she comes she comes comes comes!"

I left my body sitting against a cedar some hundred meters away, and dashed over in my light-body to make the charge aware of me. "Thirest the cogitator!" he cried. I didn't even bother shaking it off.

"I've come to converse with the mighty Fierae!" I said, feeling very good and happy in my light-body.

"You will join, I will bet!" the charge told me.

"Puny humans mustn't wager with the likes of the Fierae!" I told him.

"Ah, so cute cute, little human! No! *Fierae*-human! I see it now! You're Spearl! Ah, what a joke you've played! So cute, so cute!"

After a little more banter, two charges became one, and it was all I could do to keep from joining. "Ah, Spearl!" they cried in their crackling ecstasy. "Come join! It's been so long! Only you now, no humans left for play!"

"Maybe the New Apprentices will learn!" I said.

"Teach them, Spearl! We miss it so, cute human touch!"

"I'll try," I told them. "But tell me, how are the Fierae bearing the loss of aneke'lementals? Has it made you sad?"

"Sad?" They howled through the intensity of their joining. "Oh, no! We are not sad! We know what we do, but sometimes know not what will happen. Even the Luminae don't command the Universe!"

"Who *are* the Luminae?" I asked.

The Fierae laughed, and screamed through their ardor, "They are like fathers and we are like children!"

"The Fierae are children of the Luminae?" I asked.

"Father is not the word," they told me, "but is nearest we can say. Like heat is the offspring of the sun's light, we are. They are stars, the Luminae, and you are born of them as well. Now join, Spearl! Come share this bed of delight! Melt into our passion!"

There was just no way to say no.

Epilogue

Near the mouth of a cave overlooking the little village of Ilsa, a beautiful boy, slender and tall, stood with a fox close at his heels. He wore leather pants the color of goldenrod, and a pure white buckskin jacket. "Good to be back, isn't it, Meph?" he said to the fox.

"Beats shit out of BorderRealm and its cute little fairies," the fox replied.

The tiny lights of Ilsa's few lectric globes glimmered down in the valley. "That looks as good a place as any to start," the boy said. "Time for a little civilization! We need to teach them to annex and own! To fight for that ownership! They need to covet and provide only for their spawn—keep that wealth in the family! And *breed!* Breed, breed, breed! We need billions and billions again!"

"And *religions!*" the fox grinned. "Guilt and persecution, inquisitions and crusades and jihads! Keep them at each other's throats!"

"Ah, it will be *glorious!*" the boy crowed.

"Those Apprentices will fight you, you know."

"They're so few," the boy said, dismissing the comment.

"And HalfFire are visiting here again."

"No!" the boy lamented. "They're such a nuisance. Always keeping the humans interested in majick. They *teach* it to them, for crissakes!"

"Pain in the ass," the fox agreed.

"Oh well, we do what we can, eh Meph?"

"We do. How long do we have, anyway?"

"A time and times, whatever that means."

"The Third are about," the fox said. "So we've plenty of help. I just hope those bitchboy Seraphs stay in RealmWhite."

"Yes," the boy said. "Wouldn't want another war."

"Get our asses kicked," the fox mumbled.

"What was that?" the boy asked.

"I said, let's go! My chops are licked!"

"Mine, too!" the boy said, grinning to beat all hell.

ND - #0160 - 270225 - C0 - 229/152/11 - PB - 9781907133930 - Matt Lamination